D1479168

THE ENFORCER

RENEE ROSE

RENEE ROSE ROMANCE

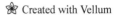 Created with Vellum

WANT FREE RENEE ROSE BOOKS?

Dressmaker's and *Her Billionaire Boss*. In addition to the free stories, you will also get bonus epilogues, special pricing, exclusive previews and news of new releases.

CHAPTER 1

O leg

Closing time at Rue's Lounge is the worst part of every week. I drain the last of my beer and set the bottle down, reluctantly rising from the table I staked out early in the night. Story, my American songbird, and her bandmates gather around the bar, still pumped with energy from another epic performance.

I hesitate, but there's no excuse to remain. Not when Rue, the mohawked owner, has already turned on the overhead fluorescents to drive the last patrons out. Not when she's specifically pointed at me and jerked her head toward the door.

I have no reason to stay. I'm not hanging around working up the nerve to ask Story out.

That would be impossible without a tongue.

I won't invent some other way to connect with her, either. I'm not the guy for her. I know that.

And I don't stay to clock more hours staring at her. Well, maybe some of that. It's pretty fucking hard to look away when she's in a room. The honey-voiced lead-singer and guitarist is magnetic. Mesmerizing. Gloriously talented and punk-beautiful.

No, I stay because I'm incapable of leaving. I can't quit the premises until I'm absolutely sure Story will get home safe.

I watch her down her third margarita in a few swift gulps and then laugh at something one of her friends says. Her Debbie Harry bob is a pale pink this week—she added a tint of champagne to her usual platinum, which makes her pale skin glow. She's so beautiful it hurts.

I force myself to walk out.

I know the bar's familiar to her, and she has lots of friends there. She also has her bandmates, which include her brother. They should all look after her. But there's alcohol involved. Possibly drugs. And I know I'm not the only *mudak* harboring wicked thoughts about what they'd like to do with the enigmatic singer of the Storytellers.

The band members sometimes stay and drink after Rue's closes, which is legal since they're on the bar's payroll. Those nights, I sit in my Yukon Denali and wait until I see Story get safely in the band's van or leave with someone she knows.

Tonight, they all head out with their groupies after me. I won't have to wait long.

Soon she'll be safely out of my sight. I can go to the penthouse and start the countdown until she plays next week over again.

I walk to my vehicle and lean my forearm on the hood, waiting to make sure she gets out of here safely.

Story weaves as she clops through the parking lot in her Doc Martens, the alcohol obviously hitting her. Her fishnets sport a tear up one thigh that makes me want to finish the job. Rip them open and lick my way to the apex of those shapely legs. Only I don't have a tongue to lick with.

Blyad'. I haven't been with a woman more than twice since it was taken from me. I don't know how I'd make love to Story without the goddamn tip of my tongue.

Her brother—the ladies man of the band—has a hot girl tucked under each arm, and he walks behind his weaving sister toward their van. His van—I think. At least, he usually drives it.

She has a tiny Smart Car she shows up in now and then.

Flynn says something to Story and veers away from the van, taking his two dates with him.

"What? Wait—Flynn—you can't!" Story hollers at his back.

He ignores her.

"I had too much to drink to drive home."

Flynn isn't even listening. He's saying something to the girls, and they're giggling in response.

The rest of their crew has scattered to other vehicles, leaving Story alone with the van.

Drunk.

Blyad'. I'm not the guy to go and tell her not to drive drunk. Again—I obviously don't—*can't*—tell anyone shit.

But I don't like it.

"Flynn!" Story calls after her brother. "Can't you drop me off first?"

"I've been drinking, too," he says although I think he's probably in far better shape than his sister.

I step away from my vehicle to show myself. I hold up my keys and point to the Denali. It's about as close as I've come to communicating in a long fucking time. I usually don't even try. That way people stop trying to connect with me. To include me. That way, I become invisible.

As much as a guy who's six-foot-six and two hundred eighty pounds can be invisible.

Story sees me and hesitates. I can tell she read my offer. She's considering it.

Part of me wants her to reject it. She shouldn't get into cars with men she doesn't really know. I mean, she knows me from a bar, but I could be any kind of creep.

But her shoulders sag in defeat. She holds her keys up and waves them at me. "Oleg—can you drive me home?" she slurs.

She wants me to drive her van.

I nod, moving before my brain has even considered the consequences.

This will require connection. Attempted conversation. Awkward silences filled most likely with avoided eye contact and the metallic scent of fear. That's what's happened before anytime someone as good as Story gets too close to me. Fuck, I hate that.

I scare the shit out of people. I'm big, menacing, covered in bratva and Siberian prison tattoos, and I can't speak because I had my tongue cut out by my last employer to keep me from spilling his secrets. I breathe intimidation. I look like I can kill a man with my bare hands without breaking a sweat.

And I have. Many times.

I'm the bratva enforcer.

Story stumbles a bit as I arrive, and I catch her elbow, steadying her. She leans into me, giving me an unfocused smile. "Thank you for rescuing me. I knew you would."

I try to ignore the effect of her words on my beating heart. The way they make it double-pump, then skip a beat, then race forward again.

4

She knew I would.

Well, good. Because I sort of figured she was one breath away from calling 911 on me for stalking because I'd been at the beautiful lead singer's shows every week for a year.

I didn't plan to become Story Taylor's stalker.

I just like to watch her perform every week. I don't know when I became obsessed. The first time I saw them play?

Nah, that was when I became a fan. When I knew I wanted to get her lithe little body underneath mine to make her scream in pleasure.

The third time?

Maybe.

All I know is she's now my addiction. I don't want to come. I fucking hate that the guys in my bratva cell figured it out and want to help me hook up with her. I want to stay invisible. A block wall no one can read. I shut down when I suddenly found myself in prison with no tongue. I learned to communicate with my fists and stopped attempting any other form of connection. But she's my weakness.

I can't stay away.

I can't stop myself from being the first one to arrive and the last one to leave on Saturday nights. I don't want to care about anything, especially not a perfect stranger who has zero interest in a giant, mute strongman.

But here I am.

Again.

Unable to look away from her beautiful face. Or stay away from that fuck-hot body that I want to pleasure every inch of. Or even think about leaving her unprotected since no one would fuck with me.

I take the keys out of her hand, open the van's passenger door, and lift her up into it with my hands at her waist. I fucking love the feel of her firm flesh under my palms. Of holding her full weight, having control of it.

"Oh!" My help startles her, and she lets out a breathy giggle. "Thanks." She's not usually wasted like this. She often nurses one drink the whole time while the rest of them get drunk. Tonight was a one-off.

I shut the door and close my eyes, willing my dick to calm the fuck down. To stop reacting like a teenage prick every time I got to touch her. She smells sweet, like margaritas and vanilla.

I know she's not mine.

She'll never be mine.

And yet some part of me refuses to understand that. Some part of me claimed her the first time I laid eyes on her.

I get in the van and start it up then look to her and shrug for directions. "Oh, um, here." She pulls out her phone and opens the Google Maps app. She enters an address, and the automated voice starts giving directions. "That's easier than me trying to tell you," she slurs. She waves a hand erratically in the air. "I might mess up or something."

I set the phone in the center console and follow the directions. Her apartment is a few miles from the bar, in a reasonable neighborhood. I find a place to park up the street, turn the van off and hand her the keys.

Now I know where she lives.

Which is a huge problem.

I purposely never followed her. That would definitely cross the line way into stalker territory. But now that I know? Fuck.

Will I be able to stay away? I'll need to know she's safe every time she leaves her apartment, not just the bar.

Goddammit.

Probably not.

This is going to be a problem for me. And her.

For both of us.

I DON'T KNOW why it doesn't occur to me until he hands me the keys that Oleg now has no way of getting home. He left his Denali at the bar!

Well, duh.

Looks like he'll have to stay the night. Ummmm… weird.

I'm not sorry. I've considered taking him home before. I mean, I was one hundred and five percent sure he'd come if I asked. He is my most devoted fan, after all.

He watches me in a way that makes me feel warm and tingly. He protects me like he's my own personal bodyguard, putting his body between me and any drunken audience members who get too close.

I get excited to play at Rue's every week knowing the big tattooed guy will be there, that he's in the audience for me. Knowing he won't take his eyes off me.

I think the only reason I never pursued it before is because then what we have would be over. It would become another one of my short-lived relationships, and we'd never be able to go back to this. And I kind of love having a silent bodyguard-slash-fan who is always there.

What if we had sex and hated it?

Then he'd stop coming. That would make him an asshole, of course, but I'm in a bubble where I can fantasize still.

Or what if he got creepy? I don't get that vibe from him,

but I'm not stupid. It's a possibility. Somehow, I feel safe with him. Somehow, I feel like he'd never hurt me.

But mostly I don't want him to become like the other guys I hook up with—date for a few months and then ditch before things get serious. My little sister says it's a safety mechanism. I leave them before they can leave me. She's probably right.

Anyway, all I know is that Oleg's different from those guys. Special.

I consider it now. Do I invite him in? Or tell him thanks for the ride and ask if he wants me to order him an Uber?

Somehow, I know if I chose the latter, he would walk away without trying anything. I mean all these months, and he's never tried once to get me to go home with him or even to hang out. He hasn't asked for my number or given me his.

He just shows up. Same time every week.

Dependable like no one else in my life has really been.

And yes, I know he can't talk to ask me out. Annie, the cocktail waitress at Rue's had told me that when he first started coming. She said he usually ordered by pointing at someone else's beer. I didn't even know he was Russian until his friends came in with him and introduced us.

And it's that realization that makes me sure he's safe. He's not going to get weird. He'd leave if I told him to leave. He'd respect the hell out of me.

I already know that because I've climbed this guy like a tree during my performances. It's one of my favorite things to do. I'll crook my finger from the stage, and he'll launch out of his seat and stand below, so I can pull a *Dirty Dancing* flying leap into his hands. Or crawl on his shoulders or fall into his arms in a honeymoon carry. I can count on the guy to catch me and carry me around while I sing. It's become part of the performance. The band members and my fans expect it now. I know Oleg would never let me fall.

"Come on," I tell him.

He hesitates, looking at me with so much suspicion it makes me laugh.

"You have to walk me to the door." I sound drunker than I am.

I blink. One second he's fifteen feet away on the other side of the van, the next he's at my elbow, steadying me when I don't walk a straight line up the sidewalk.

I unlock the door to the building.

Oleg doesn't move.

"You have to walk me all the way to my place," I tell him. "What if someone tried to mess with me in the stairwell?"

His brows slam down.

Okay, maybe I'm not as sober as I think. That sounded really stupid. "You're my bodyguard," I affirm.

It's a fact he already knows since he's self-appointed.

We walk the three flights up through the old Brownstone to my floor, and I shake out my keys to find the right one. When I get the door open, Oleg takes a step back. He's huge —wide shoulders, barrel chest, arms like tree trunks. His dark brown hair is cropped close like his beard.

"Do you want to come in?"

His heated brown gaze rakes down my body, but he shakes his head. I'm surprised how much his refusal disappoints me. I mean, I guess I thought he was a sure thing. There's no way I read this thing wrong, is there?

I face him and lean in, standing on tiptoe to throw an arm around his neck and tipping my face up to his. "Why not?"

He freezes, his big body going rigid.

If I didn't feel his erection prodding my belly, I would think he wasn't into it. But he is.

"Why are you holding back?" I whisper. I pull his head down and close my lips over his, tasting him.

He remains rigid for one second.

Two.

"Please," I ask, needing him to know I want this.

And then he surges to life. My back slams against the wall beside my door as Oleg unleashes the months of pent-up attraction between us. One beefy hand cups my ass, the other captures my nape, and he claims my mouth like it's his last chance at breathing.

My core instantly turns molten. I grind down on the leg he thrust between mine, kissing him back with as much frantic need as he's giving. I don't feel his tongue, but I use mine—probably too sloppily. He kneads my ass, helping me hump his leg.

I reach out to open my door then grab a fistful of Oleg's black t-shirt—the one stretched taut over his broad shoulders and chiseled pecs and try to tug him into my apartment.

Try is the operative word here.

Because Oleg doesn't move.

The pulse between my legs makes me antsy. "Come inside," I encourage.

He shakes his head.

What… the F?

"Oleg, come inside," I say it more like an order now. I mean, this guy's into me. He's going to give me what I need, right?

He shakes his head again then mimes drinking.

Aw, fuck.

Really?

"You won't touch me because I've been drinking?"

He nods.

He's that much of a gentleman?

"That's… sweet."

Really, really sweet.

"And annoying. Oleg, you can't do this to me," I reason, tugging fistfuls of his shirt. "That kiss just got me all hot and bothered. You can't leave me all needy. It's not fair."

His brows go down again. Jaw clenches. He wipes his lower lip with his thumb, eyes dropping to my mouth. I can see him struggling. The guy who respects me versus the guy who doesn't want to deny me. And also there's the guy who's going to have blue balls, himself. Because I felt his boner, and it was rock hard.

Like before, the moment he makes his decision, he surges into action. He crowds me backward, into my one-bedroom apartment, then kicks the door shut and locks it.

"Yes, Oleg."

I drop my purse, throw off my jacket and lunge for his lips again. We kiss like it's a contest to see who can devour the other one first. Still no tongue from him, though. Like he's too much of a gentleman for that, too. He picks me up, his forearm under my ass, and I straddle his thick trunk with my legs. He turns in a circle to get his bearings and then correctly chooses the door to my bedroom, where he takes me and drops me in the center of the bed.

The moment I'm down, he tears at the hole in my fishnets —like wrecking them was a premeditated crime—and then drags his open mouth along my inner thigh until he meets the edge of the short-shorts I wore over the fishnets. There, he bites the fabric and tugs, the heat of his breath fanning over my core.

"Eager, huh?" I ask with a laugh. He grunts in reply. That sound… fuck, it makes my pussy melt.

I race to unbutton the shorts, shoving them down my hips.

He takes over, yanking them down off my waist, along with the fishnets.

I giggle when he reaches my boots.

He makes a sound of discontent and rips at their ties. In a few seconds, I have them toed off, and I'm naked from the waist down.

Oleg grabs both my legs and pulls me down the bed. He's an aggressive lover—so different from what I'd imagined he'd be like—but I love it. I mean, I'm way into it. He nips and kisses my core but for some reason, withholds the tongue. Maybe it grosses him out to lick down there.

Instead, he sweeps one of his large fingers inside his cheek to moisten it and then rubs my entrance.

I'm already wet from the way he's handled me, and his finger slides right in.

I don't usually like being finger-fucked. Digits are too small. And not soft enough. Too pokey.

But Oleg's finger is huge. As big as a normal guy's dick. And, *oh, does he know how to use it.* He thrusts in a couple times, then pushes a second one in and starts petting my inner wall.

My mouth drops open in pleasure when he finds what must be my G-spot. My thighs twitch and slam against his broad shoulders. He strokes and circles the bundle of nerves until I'm a quivering mess, then he starts finger-fucking me hard and fast.

"Oh God," I pant, grabbing his free arm like I'm desperate to have something to hold on to while I'm on this wild ride.

He reaches under my tank top and shoves my bra cup down. I'm shocked when he pinches my nipple—hard. My hips jack off the bed in response, taking his fingers deeper.

I thrash my head on the bed, so close.

He makes a sound in the back of his throat and fucks me faster. His thumb coasts over my clit when he pumps his fingers in, and I go off like a firecracker—exploding into pleasure with my first orgasm from fingers alone.

"Oh my God!" I repeat, muscles still trembling and spasming.

Mind blown.

"That was crazy. So good." I rub the bulge of his cock in his pants. "I'm definitely ready. That was the best foreplay of my life."

But Oleg backs off the bed and shakes his head.

"Oh my God! Really?" I get up and follow him in my mostly naked state. "Why not? Because I've been drinking? I've sobered up." It feels crazy to beg for sex. Not my usual scenario. Not by a long shot.

He walks out of my bedroom into the kitchen/living area. He opens the cabinets until he finds a glass, and then he fills it with water and hands it to me.

I let out a protesting scoff, but I accept it because it's unbelievably… sweet. Is this guy for real?

The sweetness is so at odds with how rough he was in bed, and I find the combination intoxicating. Like sea salt with chocolate. You don't think they go together until you try them, and then you wonder why everything isn't sea salt-chocolate flavored. I want more of Oleg. All of him.

He looks at the glass of water then lifts his chin, crosses his arms over his chest.

"That bossy pose doesn't work on me," I tell him, fighting a smile. I want to be exasperated, but I can't be. My Russian stalker is every bit as respectful and protective as I thought he would be.

I down the entire glass of water and set it on the counter. He cocks an eyebrow as if to say, "See?"

I roll my eyes. "Are we good? You want to come back to the bedroom?"

He shakes his head but moves toward me. My limbs loosen, his nearness turning me to jelly. But then he tosses me over his shoulder, slapping my bare ass as he carries me back to the bedroom.

"Ooh!" I giggle. "Spank me, Daddy."

He stoops to pull down my covers then lays me down so carefully I want to cry. My ass tingles from the spank.

Who is this guy?

Why didn't I bring him home sooner?

He pulls the covers back and tucks me in, then brushes the backs of his fingers along my cheek, staring down at me with the same intensity he watches my show. Like I'm the only human being in the entire world. When I'm on stage, it fuels my performance. But right now, it makes my heart thump harder. It's too intimate. Slightly terrifying.

But then it's over because he walks out. I know he can't speak, but there's no nod or wave. He just leaves. I hear the front door open and close. I'm certain, without checking, that he turned the lock on the handle before shutting it to make sure I'm safe.

I pull the covers closer and curl into my pillows. "Crazy Russian," I whisper to myself, a smile on my lips. My entire body buzzes from our interlude.

I want more of him. A lot more. But I'm also already disappointed we broke the seal on our relationship because I know from experience, it won't last long. I'm the type who doesn't stick. I run as soon as things get serious. I don't know. I get this anxiety in the pit of my stomach. I consider it my inner guidance for when it's time to break things off. So I don't end up destroyed by love the way my mom always was.

And still is.

This thing will play out in a matter of weeks, the way all my relationships do, and then it will be over. And then I'll never be able to return to the pleasure of going to a gig where Oleg will be there watching. Basking in the heat of his gaze on me all night long.

Knowing there's at least one person in the crowd who is crazy about me.

Oh well. It was nice while it lasted.

CHAPTER 2

Oleg

I don't have a way to get home. I could text one of the guys in my cell, but it's almost four in the morning.

I could use a ride-sharing app, but it would mean interacting with another person—something I loathe. I decide to walk. It's only a few miles. It's freezing out, but I'm from Russia. Cold doesn't bother me, especially when I could use the temperature to cool down after what just happened.

Story's vanilla-sweet scent still lingers on my shirt.

I zip my leather jacket and shove my hands in my pockets. My mind is still filled with images of Story getting off under my hands. It was the most beautiful sight I've ever seen. Like that first hit of a drug, I'm now utterly addicted. I don't know how I'll wait a full week to see her again. How I'll settle for just watching now that I've touched her.

But I'm not stupid enough to think I can have Story.

Keep Story.

I am a man with a very dangerous past. A past that could catch up with him at any time. One that would hurt the people

17

I've come to care about—my bratva brothers—and will likely mean the end of my life.

I'm not safe for Story, even if I was lucky enough for her to want someone as broken as I am.

I back the memories up to the moment I got in the van with her, wanting to replay every minute we were together. The indulgence costs me.

Dearly.

Because I don't notice anyone else around.

Pain explodes on the back of my head as I'm clubbed from behind. A bag gets pulled over my face as I topple forward, landing heavily on one knee. I try to rip it off, to see my attackers, but the blow to my skull disorients me, and I tumble to my side before I yank it away.

The cold metal of a gun presses against my temple. "Don't move." The words are Russian.

Blyad'.

They found me.

I always knew this day would come. I knew it, but to have it happen tonight—the night I got to watch my little *lastochka* come—makes it a special torture. The night I'm given a burning reason to live.

"Get up," a different voice rasps.

"You want him not to move or to get up?" a third voice argues. "He doesn't look that smart. Why confuse the guy?"

Yeah, every *mudak* thinks he's a comedian.

Several thoughts snap together in my brain. If they wanted me dead—if they worked for Skal'pel'—I'd already be dead. So that means these idiots work for someone who's after Skal'pel'. Someone who wants what's in my head. Which means they have orders to take me alive.

The crack I took to the skull makes it hard to focus, but I'm a big guy. I can still throw my weight. I stand, launching myself backward into the guy holding the gun. As I predicted, he doesn't shoot.

I knock him on his back, my weight landing square in his middle. His gun arm splays out to the side, but I miss snatching the pistol before it clatters to the ground out of reach.

I rip the hood off my head and turn to punch him in the face to make sure he stays down then go for the gun. Too late —it has already been scooped up by *Mudak #2*.

"Shoot him in the kneecap!" *Mudak #3*—the comedian—suggests. These guys would never make it anywhere in Ravil's cell. They lack the organization and discipline of bratva. And intelligence.

Mudak #2 does try to shoot me in the fucking knee. My fist hits his throat at the same time he pulls the trigger. The bullet grazes my leg. At least I hope that's just a graze. I feel a burning line all along my outer thigh.

The gun clatters to the ground.

Lights come on from the windows in the buildings all around us. Someone shouts down that he's called the police.

"What in the fuck are you doing?" *Mudak #1* is conscious again. "You're not supposed to shoot him."

I'm still trying to get to the gun—a mistake—when I feel a sharp jab to the back of my neck.

A fucking needle!

They tranqued me. I have to work fast. I spin and backhand *Mudak #1* in the temple. He staggers, and I punch his mouth with my left fist, then his nose with my right, then his jaw with the left again, and he's down.

The world is already starting to spin. I can't tell if it's because of the head injury or the drugs or both. I have to get away before I black out.

I forget about the gun and my aspirations of eliminating

these guys. The cops are on their way, and there're a few dozen witnesses looking through their windows now. The two upright assholes try to wrestle me to the ground at the same time, which gives me the advantage. I hook the throat of one of them with my hand and spin him around to knock the head with the other guy. Four more punches, and they're on the sidewalk.

My vision's fading around the edges. I stagger, limp-running in the direction of Story's building. I won't make it, though. I just need to find a place to hide before I pass out. Before the cops arrive.

Are those sirens?

My vision has streaks in it. I can't focus. I stumble and fall against something. A car.

No, a van.

Fuck, it's the van. Could it be Story's van?

I fumble with the back door, but my fingers don't work.

Or maybe it's because it's locked.

No, my fingers work now. The door opens. I was an idiot for not making sure it was locked when we got here. The inside is packed with amps and speakers. The sound system. Story's guitar. I don't even know how it's possible I found the van.

The miracle that it would be unlocked. There's no room—especially not for a big guy like me, but I climb in anyway.

I'm not sure if I make it all the way in. I definitely don't get the door closed. I pass out, face down over the speakers, my head splitting with pain.

STORY

I dream I'm onstage at Rue's. Oleg's watching me from

his usual table in front of the stage. I'm performing for everyone, but his attention is the fuel behind my act. He gives me courage to be crazy—go big. I feel more like myself under his watchful gaze. The noise of the crowd fades away, and I come alive. I can be more of myself.

Only this time, something happens. A bunch of girls come up on stage and distract my brother in the middle of the set. I'm pissed at him for being such a man-whore and letting his womanizing get in the way of the band. I'm pissed enough that I shove the mic back on the stand and flip everyone off.

The audience gets crazy, yelling at me to go on. Or maybe they're yelling at Flynn, I can't tell. All of it pisses me off.

And then Oleg's there at the front of the stage. He lifts his arms, and I jump, trusting he'll catch me. His large hands span my waist, and he easily lifts me down to the floor, then he takes my guitar from me, tosses me over his shoulder, and smacks my ass as he walks out the door.

I wake up, a naughty-girl smile curling my lips.

Oleg did that. Last night.

He threw me over his shoulder and smacked my ass. Then put me to bed.

Why does that memory get me even more wet than the orgasm he gave me? There was also the way he shoved me against the door and palmed my pussy like he owned it.

Oleg has a dommy side. My large guy is larger-than-life in bed, too. Maybe it's his way of speaking. If you'd asked me yesterday what I liked, I never in a million years would've named that. I date musicians. Artists. Soft, articulate boys who smoke pot and philosophize about the environment and social justice. Things I care about, too.

I date guys who are like myself. Or like my younger, not-so-little brother. It's a familiar type. Guys who seem to fit with me. With my friends. With my bohemian lifestyle.

Not guys like Oleg. Never giant, tattooed, Russian men with chivalrous, but extremely dominant manners.

But I freaking *loved* the way he touched me.

I'm embarrassed that I tried to get him to have sex with me and peeved he refused.

And I'm also kind of mad he didn't leave his number or ask for mine.

But he'll be there next week.

I know it with certainty. He's been there every week for the last year. And he comes for me.

And all these thoughts about Oleg still don't negate my saddest one—now that we've started down this path, we're on the road to the end. Because that's how things roll for me. I don't do long-term relationships. I don't like to rely on people because I've learned through experience, they always let me down. My parents loved me—deeply—but I sure as hell couldn't count on either one of them to ever be there for me when I needed them. My mom was always a hot mess, and my dad was often swept away with partying and women —same as Flynn, now. I won't

I get out of bed, happy to discover I'm not the slightest bit hungover.

I should shower and eat breakfast, but all I want to do is get my guitar. Oleg tickled my muse, and I need to play. Maybe actually compose for once. It's been eighteen months since I've written an original song.

I pull on a pair of pajama pants and boots and throw a jacket over the top I'm still wearing from last night. The keys to the band's van are right by the door because Oleg is a freaking prince.

I leave my door unlocked and trot down the stairs and out the front door.

The March morning air is frigid, and I yank my jacket

closed as I look around for the van. I find it a half-block down. When I get to it, though, I gasp. My heart starts pounding with a surge of adrenalin.

Oh God.

Fuck, fuck, fuck.

Some fucking asshole has broken into the van. The back gate is slightly ajar! All our sound equipment was in there. And my guitar! Flynn will freak out. I'm freaking out.

Cringing, I swing the door open.

And gasp a second time.

"Oleg?"

Oh my God. Oleg is face down over the equipment. One of his pant legs is soaked with blood. Holy shit—is he dead?

I touch his ankle and find his skin cold. Christ, he could have frozen to death last night.

Did he?

I throw myself inside and tug at his massive body, pulling his arm and trying to move him.

He stirs.

"Oh thank God. I thought you were dead. Oleg?"

He barely lifts his head, groans. I'm not sure he even recognizes me.

"Oh my God. What happened to you? I need to get you to a hospital."

That seems to rouse him because he instantly surges up, hitting his head on the top of the van. He groans and drops it into both his hands, sitting on a speaker.

"Come on, I'll drive you to a hospital."

He grunts this time and shakes his head *no*.

"No? You don't want to go?"

A very emphatic no because his bloodshot eyes meet mine and hold. I mean, it couldn't be clearer. He doesn't want to go to a hospital.

"Why not? Are you… an illegal? Are you afraid of being deported?"

He shakes his head again and lurches forward, stumbling down out of the van. He drops to one knee and then on his side to one shoulder in pain.

"Oleg, you're bleeding. I don't know how much you've already lost. I need to get you help."

No.

I swear I can almost hear the word in my head, he projects it so loudly. He struggles back up to his feet, shaking his head.

Tears of frustration spike my eyes. I'm not the type to just override someone's wishes, but I'm also not sure he's capable of making a sound decision right now. "What happened to you?" I ask again, which is stupid because I know he can't speak.

I arrive at the only other option that makes sense. "You have to come inside. Can you make it?"

He steps forward, but his leg gives out. His face contorts in obvious pain. He looks down at the blood-soaked fabric like he's surprised.

Then he scans the area, even though I'm not sure he can even focus.

I slam the van doors and lock them then tuck myself against his side, pulling his arm around my shoulders, so I can support him. "Let's go. We'll get you to my place, okay?"

He allows me to lead him into the building.

It takes forever to get him up three flights of stairs. I'm nearly in tears the whole time because he's in a ton of pain, a little groan escaping him with each hard jostle. Thankfully, none of my neighbors pick this time to go up or down the stairs because I'd have a hard time explaining. And somehow,

I get the feeling that whatever happened to Oleg isn't something he wants the authorities to know about.

When we get to the last flight of stairs, Oleg faceplants against the wall when he loses his balance.

I cry out for him and grab his arm tight. "Oleg, you can do it. We're almost there. This is my floor. Just a few more steps."

He hobbles up them, and I push open the door.

"Come here." I bring him into the bathroom. "I need to get you cleaned up."

He leans against the door like he's weak. No—like he's dizzy.

"Did you get hit on the head?"

He reaches his hand behind his head and winces when his fingers touch it.

"Oleg," I moan. This time the tears spill.

Oleg's head jerks up when I sniff and alarm passes over his expression. He reaches out, his thumb roughly wiping a tear from my cheek.

"No—it's okay. I'm just crying for you. I don't know what happened, and I'm scared for you. And I feel bad that you're hurting."

Oleg's brows knit. He's breathing hard from the trek up the stairs. He catches my face in both his hands and brings his forehead down to mine. We pant together, our breath mingling. His skin is cold against mine. God, he must have hypothermia by now!

After a moment, after his breathing slows, he presses his lips to my forehead.

I blink rapidly, still fighting off the urge to cry. "Let's get you out of these bloody jeans." I unbutton his jeans and pull down the zipper.

He leans his hip against the bathroom cabinet—I'm

guessing because he can't stand up on his own—and lets me pull them down. He doesn't hiss or flinch when I get to his wound, but I'm sure it hurts.

A chunk of flesh seems to be missing. There's a hole in his jeans above it. "What caused this? A bullet?"

Oleg doesn't confirm with a nod or shake, but I'm sure I'm right. Not that I've seen a bullet wound before, but this has to be what it is.

"I think you got lucky," I tell him. I don't think the bullet hit anything. I doubt it's still inside him. It seems like it just nicked the side of his leg.

His jeans are sticky and stiff with blood, which makes them harder to remove, but I manage to get them down to his feet, then I help him toe out of his boots, so I can get them all the way off.

"Um, I'm thinking of a bath to clean the blood off and warm you up." I look at the wound. Maybe that's a bad idea. "Or does that sound terrible?"

He takes off his jacket and shirt, which I take to mean he's on board.

I turn on warm water and plug the drain then help him get his shirt off.

His chest is gorgeous—a solid muscle dusted with hair and covered in tattoos. They creep up his neck and all the way down his arms. They're markings of some kind. A rose on his chest. A manacle on one wrist. A dagger with drops of blood. If I didn't know with total certainty that Oleg is safe for me, I would find his appearance intimidating. I imagine that's what he's going for.

I want to trace the lines of every one of them and find out what they mean, but now's not the time. I hook my thumbs in the waistband of his boxers and pull them down to the floor.

Oleg's cock lengthens before my eyes, and I try to ignore it. It's a beautiful hard-on, but this is so not the right time.

I take his big arm to help him to the bathtub. He steps into the water carefully, throwing a hand out to catch the wall, like he got dizzy again, and then slowly sinks into the water with a groan.

"Oleg," I whisper brokenly.

I could never be a nurse. It freaking kills me to see him damaged like this. I feel dizzy and woozy just watching him deal with it. Like my body experiences his pain.

He leans his head back against the tile and closes his eyes. I'm not sure if he passed out or not. Whether I should wake him. Don't they say with concussions, you should keep the person awake? Of course, I found him unconscious in the van, so that train probably already boarded.

The water turns an orange-pink from the blood. I get a washcloth to clean off his leg, gently wiping around the wound, but avoiding touching it. I will pour alcohol on it when he gets out.

I'm on my knees beside the bath, all wrapped up in trying to figure out what to do for him when his hand settles on my back. I look up and find his lids open by a fraction. He strokes my hip.

He's soothing me. Or maybe thanking me. It's hard to be sure. I guess it doesn't matter—the energy is the same.

"I'm sorry this happened to you," I say, my voice getting rough at the end. "I hope it wasn't because you drove me home."

He shakes his head, and his fingers squeeze my side.

"Do you know who did this to you?"

His gaze shifts to the tile wall. He's ignoring my question. I get the feeling he does that a lot. Being mute lets him opt out of conversation.

A loud jangle from the floor startles me. It's Oleg's phone. His expression registers alarm. I lunge for it, thinking it might be important and find it in his jeans pocket.

The screen reads something in Russian letters. "Do you want to get this?"

He snatches it from my hand, and I think it must be important, but then he smashes the phone against the lip of the tub three times until it shatters into dozens of pieces.

My mouth drops open, and I jerk back at the sudden violence of the movement.

Oleg notices and holds up his hands, as if to show he's no threat to me.

"Jesus," I whisper, still shocked. "What's going on?"

He catches my hand and brings it to his lips, kissing my fingers softly before letting it go. That's a thank you. Or maybe an apology. He's showing me there will be no violence toward me.

I pull his hand to my own mouth and return the gesture. "I'm going to get you some ibuprofen, okay? Are you all right here?"

He nods.

I do a quick safety check and decide he's too big to drown in the tub, even if he passes out while I'm gone, then leave.

When I come back, I bring a glass of blueberry juice I had in the refrigerator because I figure he probably hasn't put anything in his belly since the beer he drank last night.

He seems to be passed out again.

"Oleg?"

He doesn't stir. His head lols to the side like he's out cold.

I set the juice and ibuprofen down on the counter, my heart picking up speed again. "Oleg? Are you okay?" I put one hand on his shoulder, the other cupping his face and lifting it upright.

He makes a sound, but it seems to take great effort for him to open his eyes. When he does, it takes a while for him to focus on my face.

I check the back of his head, where he rubbed before. He doesn't have a huge bump, but there is a two-inch cut, as if whatever hit him struck so hard it split the skin on impact. I feel like I've heard that where concussions are involved, you want to have a goose egg. The lack of a goose egg is more of a problem.

I don't like that he doesn't have a bigger bump. I make a note to Google it and also to bring him an ice pack for it. And alcohol.

"Here, can you take this ibuprofen?" I hold out my hand up to his mouth to drop them in.

He doesn't move.

"Open," I order.

He still doesn't move.

"It's just ibuprofen, see?" I open my palm to show him the three pills. "I have Tylenol if you prefer that."

He opens his lips a tiny bit. Not enough for me to be able to drop the pills in.

"Open more, Oleg."

His jaw opens a bit wider and shock flashes through my body like a lightning strike. I suddenly understand why he didn't want to open his mouth, and I want to bawl like a baby.

Oleg is missing his tongue.

Oh God.

Part of his tongue. It looks like someone cut it in half. *That's* why he can't talk.

It's all I can do to not show my shock. To not drop to my knees and weep for him. But I hold back my sob and drop the pills in his mouth then hand him the juice glass. He drips water on the floor when he lifts his hand to take the glass and swallows down the entire contents of the glass.

"Do you want more? Or something to eat?"

He shakes his head. His eyes are already closed.

"Hey, let me get you out of there before you pass out again. I don't like the idea of you lying in cold water."

His eyes crack, but he doesn't move. I push up my sleeve and dip my hand in the water, reaching for the plug.

His butt's in the way. I slide my palm around the curve. "Move over."

He groans as he moves, and I pull the drain.

"Okay, now I'm really worried about getting you out of there. Please say you can stand up?"

He leans his head back against the wall and closes his eyes.

"Oleg. Can you get out of the tub?"

He nods without opening his eyes.

"I'm sorry. I just want to get you into my bed before you pass out again. Okay?"

Another nod.

Still no cracked lids.

"Please?"

Water splashes as he moves abruptly. It's like he was marshalling his strength for the move. He lumbers to stand, catching the wall with his hand again.

I slide the bath rug to meet the place his foot is going to land when he steps out then jump beside him, so he can lean on me if he needs to.

He makes it out without toppling, thank God. I grab a towel from the rack. "Hang on just a second." I hurriedly dry him off, taking care not to knock him off balance. He holds the wall, his expression a stoic mask. I do a half-assed job, but it's better than him getting the bed wet. I wrap the towel around his waist and then wrap my arm firmly behind his back. "Okay, let's get you to my room."

I get him in there and fall down on the bed with him, trying to get him in it. He rolls onto his side and groans. I curl up, facing him, staring at his pained expression, unwilling to leave him.

He watches me watching him. Time lengthens. Stands still. I don't know how long I stay there. Long after his eyes close, and he passes out. I curl my hand into his, holding his fingers, wishing I knew what to do.

CHAPTER 3

O^{leg}

Oleg

I wake not sure how long I've been out. I shove the covers off and attempt to sit up. I wait until the room stops spinning and my stomach stops lurching before I focus and look around. I'm naked, but there's a gauze bandage taped to my leg, covering the bullet wound, and my clothes are folded neatly on a chair. Story must've dressed my wound and washed the clothes for me at some point. I pull on my t-shirt, almost falling to the floor in agony when the neckhole passes over the bruise on my head. I take my time putting on my boxer briefs, not trusting myself to stand yet.

I'm guessing I've been out of it for at least twenty-four hours, considering I woke during the night, and now it's light again. And it was morning when Story found me. I think.

Story. She's been in and out of the room, bringing me more ibuprofen and juice. I have a vague recollection of her lying beside me during the night, but that could've just been a fantasy. Every time I woke, the usual adrenaline pumped through my veins, my normal agitation of existence revved up, but then I remembered where I was—not in prison, not in my own room, but in Story's apartment, and the noisiest place inside me quieted.

Being near my little *lastochka*—my swallow—soothes a lifetime of struggle.

I know it won't last. I know I can't remain here forever. I need to figure out who's after me and what they want. Eliminate them.

I smashed my phone thinking they might have put a tracker in it although in my more lucid moments, I realize they aren't that sophisticated. They're not like my *pakhan* Ravil's bratva cell. I highly doubt they have someone like Dima who can hack anything. Or a Fixer like Maxim. They didn't seem organized or high-tech.

They are idiot criminals unprepared for the job they were sent to do.

I'm not dumb enough to think whoever sent them won't rectify his mistake the next time, though. And that brings on sharp realization.

Those guys were waiting for me. Which means they might know where Story lives.

No... maybe not. They would've been waiting outside the door.

The van.

They must've followed the van. My brain is so fucking fuzzy it's hard to think this through. Maybe they got behind in traffic, but then spotted it again after I'd parked?

That has to be it.

I lunge off the bed, a hoarse cry coming out of my throat. Fuck. I hate it when I make noise.

Story runs from her small living area and meets me at the doorway to the bedroom. She's barefoot, looking gorgeous in leggings and a long dusty rose sweater that falls off one shoulder, exposing her pale skin and delicate collar bones.

She isn't wearing her usual heavy eyeliner and stage makeup, and she's even more alluring fresh-faced.

"What is it? Are you okay?"

I look around wildly for the keys to the van. Every turn of my head makes the apartment spin. The pounding in my skull makes me want to chop it off my neck. I spot her purse by the door and point.

Story looks over her shoulder, searching. "What is it?"

I clomp past her, stumbling when the floor dips and my feet seem to slide off the surface. I catch myself on the sofa and keep going. When I reach her purse, I root through it, relieved when I find the keys there. I hold them up and point outside.

"You want me to take you somewhere?"

Blyad'.

I shake my head.

"You want to drive?" she asks dubiously.

I nod. I need to move that van. But moving my head makes a wave of nausea climb up my throat. Great. I'm dizzy, and now I need to puke.

"Here!" Story runs and grabs a notebook and pen then brings them back to me.

Fuck.

"Write it," she encourages.

I hate myself for never bothering to learn the Roman alphabet. Ravil requires his men to only speak English in the penthouse. He wants everyone in his cell to speak it perfectly, to make sure we blend in and avoid discrimination. So I understand it completely. But I, of course, was exempt from speaking it, so I also made myself exempt from learning to write it. Stupid, stupid mistake.

Frustrated, I snatch the pen up and write in Russian, "Move the van."

She stares at the words. "Shit. You don't write in English."

I shake my head. If I hadn't busted my phone I could find a translation app to help us right now, but I already screwed that up.

"Fuck!"

I take the pen and draw a terrible rendering of the van and the street outside. Then I draw a few more streets. I drag a penline from the van down the street and over a few blocks and then make an X.

"You want to move the van."

Relief pours through me. *Gospodi,* how did she even figure that out? I swear the girl can read my mind. She's magical.

I grip both her shoulders to show how important it is and nod.

"Got it." She grabs the keys from me then takes her coat off the rack by the door.

I catch her arm and shake my head, pointing at my chest. I can't have her move the van. What if someone is out there?

"You aren't going anywhere. You can barely stand," she tells me. "I'll be right back. Let me get you to the sofa."

Dammit. I can't let her go for me. I reach for the keys, but she dances out of my reach, and the room spins around me.

"Okay, I'm going before you kill yourself trying to stop me. Be back in a minute."

I groan and make my way to the window to look out. I'm relieved when she makes it to the van safely and pulls out.

Only then do I find my way to the couch where I collapse and breathe into the nausea. The couch is old but comfortable. Story's place is nice. Not fancy but very comfortable. It's an old building. The ceilings are high with old-fashioned molding, and the floors are oak. They could use a refinishing, but they've worn well. There's real art on the walls. Not expensive matching art but a random assortment of paintings, framed photographs and poems. Like she lives in a world of artists who all contributed something to her place.

Story returns fifteen minutes later and tosses her bag and coat on the rack by the door. "Done. You want something to eat?"

I shake my head.

"You haven't had anything but a little juice in twenty-four hours. I think you need to try to eat."

I don't answer. At home I rarely communicate with my cell brothers. They're used to my blank expressions, and they don't try to talk to me unless it's important. Sasha, our fixer Maxim's new bride, tries sometimes. But this thing with Story is fucking painful. She keeps asking questions, watching me for answers. Trying to connect.

It triggers the rage and frustration I thought I buried long ago, back in prison. After I woke up without a tongue, framed for a crime I didn't commit.

Story goes to the kitchen—which is really just one wall of the living area with a two-person breakfast bar to separate the space. She opens the refrigerator and rummages through, eventually returning with a container of lemon yogurt that she opened and sprinkled granola on top.

"Do you like yogurt? Russians are supposed to like yogurt, right?" she cringes like she just said something stupid, so I take it from her, even though I have no interest in eating.

I force a few bites down before I set it on her 1970's coffee table.

"I teach lessons all afternoon," Story says. She looks apologetic, so I struggle to figure out what she's telling me. "Like, here, in the living room."

I grunt and throw myself off the couch and onto my feet. My head aches so badly I can't see straight, but I stumble for the bedroom and miraculously land in the center of her bed.

I can't put my thoughts together well enough to decide if I should use Story's phone to text Ravil. I'm almost positive my *pakhan* and cell brothers have nothing to do with this shit. They wouldn't sell me out. They have no reason to.

But they don't know I worked for Skal'pel'. That I've seen the faces of people he operated on—before and after. And if they found out, they might not forgive me for the omission. My work fell on the other side of the Moscow bratva, where most of my bratva brothers originated. Some of Skal'pel's clients were hiding from Igor Antonov, the now deceased *pakhan*. Sasha's father. I helped them change their identities and disappear. I may recognize their new faces. People would either pay a lot of money for that information or kill me to keep it quiet.

I have often wondered why I'm still alive. Why Skal'pel' dumped me in a prison instead of a cedar box.

It's a mystery that haunts me. All these years, I've been waiting for the other shoe to drop. For someone to show up and finish the job.

Looks like it's finally happening.

So even if my cell doesn't forsake me for what I've done, I can't bring this shit down on them. It's not their problem. I need to handle it on my own.

That's what I decide, anyway, before the pounding in my head makes me pass out again.

STORY

Oleg sleeps in my bedroom all morning and into the

38

afternoon. I change the dressing on his wound, pouring hydrogen peroxide on it. Thankfully, it really doesn't look that bad, not that I have any experience with bullet wounds. But it's not deep and appears more like a friction burn than anything.

I'm more worried about the presumed concussion.

And about whatever shit Oleg's in. He's badly injured, and I have no idea who did it or what happened. I have people showing up for music lessons here all afternoon and a wounded guy who may have men looking for him in my bedroom.

What if someone shows up here for him? He's pretty incapacitated. I would have to protect him, and I don't even know if I'm capable of that. Violence isn't really in my wheelhouse.

And a much smaller but still realistic concern—what if he needs my help while I'm trying to give lessons? It would be unprofessional and hard to explain why there's a giant, bleeding and dizzy man in my bedroom.

Fortunately, he sleeps through the guitar lessons I give all afternoon. I've already seen five regular students when a new student, Jeff Barnes, shows up. I got a bit of a creeper vibe from him on the phone. My mom's told me a hundred times that she doesn't like me teaching lessons out of my own apartment, but I don't really have another choice. Leasing a music studio would eat up every cent I make with the lessons, which are how I pay the rent and eat.

When he called for lessons he played cool, doing that thing where he acted like we're friends. He dropped a few names of people I know and said he likes to watch the Story-tellers play. Sounded enthusiastic. I figured he either wants in the band or he wants in my pants. Still, fifty bucks is fifty bucks, and lessons are how I pay the rent, so I scheduled him.

I didn't get a dangerous vibe from him, and now that I've met him in person, I still don't.

But the guy is annoying. He's definitely not here to learn guitar. He acts like he already knows everything I'm trying to teach him, even though he doesn't, and keeps trying to make small-talk instead of learn.

At the end of his half-hour, I put my guitar down. "Okay, time's up." I don't offer to schedule another lesson because I didn't enjoy teaching him. If he asks, fine. But I'm not going to try to get him into a regular package or anything.

He makes no move to get up off my couch. Instead, he pulls a little baggie out of his jacket pocket and starts rolling a joint.

For fuck's sake.

I don't happen to have any students after him because it's already 6:30—my dinner time—but I easily could have. Maybe I'll pretend I do.

"You want a hit?" he offers after flicking his tongue along the edge of the rolling paper.

"No, I'm good. And listen, I've got plans for dinner, so…"

"Yeah." But the asshole doesn't take the hint. He just flicks his lighter and lights up in my living room.

I'm not the type to pitch a bitch. Sounds like we know some of the same people, and I don't want to completely be rude. I get up and start cleaning the kitchen to give him a better hint.

I look over to see him watching me with hooded eyes.

Ugh. Definitely a creeper.

And then behind him, in the doorway of the bedroom, Oleg appears. He's put on his jeans, and he still looks pale, but his focus is on the back of Jeff's head, and his expression is deadly.

"Oh hey, honey," I chirp brightly to call Jeff's attention to Oleg's presence.

The guy whips around in surprise, coughing on the hit he just took.

Oleg folds his arms across his massive chest. He's huge, and he looks like he could rip Jeff's head off his shoulders with one hand. I notice, only because I'm looking for it, that he's also strategically propped himself up against the door-frame for balance.

He's playing along for me, just like he always does at my show when I decide to climb him like a jungle gym or make him carry me around on his shoulders. Or catch me when I dive from the stage.

I wrinkle my nose at Jeff apologetically. "My boyfriend doesn't really like when guys hang around past their lessons."

I've never seen a guy move so fast. Jeff shoves his pot back in his jacket pocket and slams his ratty guitar case closed. He's out the door with only one side of it buckled and his jacket dragging on the floor as he carries it under his arm.

As soon as the door shuts, I laugh and skip over to Oleg, reaching on tiptoe to give him a peck on the cheek. "Thank you," I purr. "You're a good bodyguard."

Brows still down, he frowns at the door.

"He would've left if I'd told him to," I reassure him, guessing at his thoughts. "But now he'll never overstay." I reward Oleg with a big smile.

Oleg casts another dark glance at the door.

"I know, you would've beat him up for me if I needed you to, right?"

Oleg draws his index finger across his throat. A shiver runs down my spine because I believe the threat. As gentle and safe as Oleg seems to me, as much as I think of him as my giant teddy bear, I have every reason to believe he's a criminal—a dangerous criminal. Those tattoos tell a story of violence. And he runs in a group of Russian guys who all have tattoos like his. They're Russian mafiya, probably. I don't even want to know what kind of crimes they're into. I mean, I found Oleg shot in the back of my van.

"Okay, that won't be necessary," I tell Oleg, sober now.

He still looks ready to kill someone.

"Seriously. It's good to know that, ah, you're willing to kill for me, but I wouldn't want that. *Ever*." I'm trying to be as clear about this as I can.

Oleg seems to catch my tone because a flash of uncertainty replaces the deadly expression, and he runs a tattooed hand over his stubbled face.

"Is that what you do?" I don't know where I worked up the nerve to ask. I really don't think I want to hear the answer. I bring my fingertips to touch the place across his breastbone where I saw the dagger tattoo. "That's what the ink means, right?"

He gives me a single nod.

Fuck. A violent shiver runs through me. I definitely didn't want to know that.

"Is that why you got attacked? Someone's after you now?"

He tips his head to the side, considering my question, then shakes it.

Okay, so he didn't get attacked as a retaliation over murder. Good to know. Again, I'm stupid for asking.

The less I know about Oleg and his crimes, the better.

For a second time, a wave of regret runs through me about getting to know Oleg better. He's definitely not the kind of guy to make a boyfriend, not that I ever last more than a month or two with boyfriends, anyway. Now we're headed

42

down the path toward this thing ending, and I don't want it to end. And I didn't want it to change.

Except that's a lie. Because I haven't been able to stop thinking about the rough way Oleg took me—and he didn't even *take me*-take me! But I still feel his hands on me. The way he shoved me up against the wall and palmed my pussy like he owned it. The way he ripped open my fishnets to get to my skin. That bald hunger in him. The dominance.

I crave more of it. I'm definitely seeing this thing through. I want all the sex I can get before it ends.

But end, it must.

Endings are a given with any guy, and Oleg's profession makes it a certainty.

Which is too bad. Because I like the way I feel with him. Like I can be me.

All of me. Unfiltered me.

It's just easy with him. Even with the communication disrupt.

I like Oleg. I press my body against his, asking for an embrace. Like always, he gives me what I ask for. I bite his giant pectoral muscle—only because it seems so inviting.

He surprises me by fisting my hair and tugging my head back. He lowers his mouth slowly, watching me intently, like he's looking for a sign of displeasure. I lift my lips. He brushes his across my mouth twice, then nips my lower lip. Then his fingers release my hair to cup the back of my head, holding me in place for a real kiss. A demanding kiss.

I miss the tongue—my heart fucking bleeds for Oleg and his injured tongue—but even without it, it's a better kiss than I've had from any guy, hands down.

It's the energy behind it. That raw, rough desire. That sensation of being both claimed and honored at the same time. It makes my knees weak.

Unfortunately, it has the same effect on Oleg. No, that's probably the concussion. He stumbles a bit and breaks the kiss, catching the wall.

"It's okay. You should probably lie back down. But you owe me," I warn him.

He cocks his head, like he requires an explanation.

I run my hands across his chest and down his washboard abs. "I'm going to need some of this before you go."

Oleg tugs me by the nape back up to his face and gives me a soft, exploratory kiss. Heat flares everywhere. I want him now, but I know that's impossible. When he pulls away, I bring both hands to cup his face. "Can you eat some more food?"

He hesitates, then shakes his head, turning back to the bedroom.

"I'll bring you some more pain killers," I tell him.

He doesn't acknowledge my words, but when I bring him the ibuprofen, he downs the pills obediently and drinks the whole glass of juice, same as every time. I push away the creeping anxiety that I should've taken him to the hospital.

Oleg

Story's scent surrounds me. I dream I'm grinding against her ass, one hand possessively cupping her breast.

No, not a dream.

I blink in the morning light. I'm in my little *lastochka*'s bed with a raging hard-on shoved between her legs like a heat-seeking missile going for home.

She's awake. I know because she pushes her ass back against my lap and moans softly. I pinch and rub her nipple between my thumb and forefinger, pluck it into a stiff peak.

My hand is under her tank top—apparently it sleep-walked there. My dick is still in my briefs, fortunately.

I've never wanted to speak so badly. Fourteen years since my tongue was clipped, and this is the moment that gives me the most pain. Because I have all manner of dirty-talk swimming in my head, and I don't have a way to get it out. To check in with her. Make sure she wants to get what I want to give.

But she told me earlier, didn't she? She made it clear what she wanted.

I bite her neck and slip my hand down her belly and into her pajama bottoms. She opens her knee for me. I suck in a breath when my fingers stroke past her silky landing strip and over her slit. She isn't wearing panties, and she's hot and wet for me. I run the pad of my finger through her juices, dragging them up to swirl around her clit. It stiffens and lengthens under my touch.

The memory of making her come the last time gets me harder than stone. I want to take my time with her now, but I fear I won't have the finesse. Not with my head still aching and my stamina so low.

I catch her throat with my other hand and pull her head back to my shoulder as I slide my finger over her sex, listening to her little gasps and mewls.

You want me to touch you here? To make you come? Or do you need my cock?

I wish I could fucking ask her. But I can't, so I use my fingers to please her. I circle her clit until she squirms, her little whimpers growing more desperate, then I screw one inside her. I love the way her legs clamp closed, and her hand presses down over the top of mine.

"Your fingers are as big as some guys' cocks," she moans.

I love that she's dirty-talking, but mentioning other guys' dicks makes me want to kill every guy she's ever been with.

"You're not going to hold out on me this time, are you?" She rocks her hips taking my finger deeper.

Aw, fuck.

Now she's getting it.

I slip my finger out and sit up.

Story sits up, too. "What?"

Okay, I was working up the strength to climb out of bed for a condom. But I remember she set my wallet on her night-stand when she washed my jeans. I point to it, and she snatches it up. "Condom?" She sounds breathless.

I love when she reads my mind.

I take the wallet, flip it open, and pull out the condom.

"Let me help." She pushes me to my back. I hide my wince when my tender head hits the pillow. I'm too fasci-nated by my *shalun'ya*—my bad girl—to care about the pain. She straddles my legs, ripping the condom wrapper open with her teeth.

I tug the hem of her tank top twice and lift my chin. I'm being demanding, but I can tell she likes it because a naughty smile curls her lips, and she whips it off over her head and throws it to the floor.

Ah, those glorious tits. Her nipples are pale—peach tipped—and sweet, making the sight of her breasts feel like an unexpected gift.

She pulls my briefs down to free my erection and wraps her hand around the base. "Wow." She sounds impressed. "It's, ah, definitely bigger than your finger."

I hold up my hand for comparison, and she smiles, her gaze lingering on my face.

"I didn't expect you to be quite so…"

I go still, worried about what she's going to say.

"...*aggressive*. It was hot."

It takes a couple seconds for me to get over thinking it was a complaint. I hadn't meant to be so dominant, but it had been hard to hold back all my pent-up desire for her. Story's been my obsession for a long time now. But to hear she liked it, that she wants that, makes the motor inside me roar to life. Whatever stamina I was afraid I didn't have appears. I could fuck this girl all night long if it was night.

Which it isn't.

She lowers her head and slides her mouth over the tip of my cock. My head nearly explodes with pleasure. And pain. But the *pleasure.* I groan out loud, surprising myself because I generally try to stop myself from letting any sound emerge.

Story slides her mouth down and up again, raising gooseflesh all over my skin. She pins her gaze to mine watching the havoc she wreaks as she takes me into her mouth again and again.

It's all too much. I've waited too long for this moment without ever believing it would happen. And fuck, I'm not going to come in her mouth. Not when she told me plainly that she wants me to give it to her hard.

I grip my own dick, which makes her pop off. I pull her pajama bottoms off. I want to put my mouth on her dripping cunt, but I have more confidence about what I can do with my cock. Not having a tongue to please her fucking killed me last time.

You'd think after so long I'd have accepted my fate. I'm not a wallowing fuck, but Story awakens the need to be so much more than what I've been for the last years—barely half a man.

She props herself up on her forearms to watch me roll the condom on. She liked me aggressive, so I grab her thighs and tug her to the center of the bed, showing off my strength.

Her breathy laugh makes it so worth it. "Ooh, there's Big Daddy."

Big Daddy. I don't know enough American pop culture to be sure I understand the moniker, but I get the gist. She's my *shalun'ya,* and I'm the guy in charge. The guy who's going to fuck her until she screams.

I position myself between her open thighs and rub the head of my sheathed cock over her slit. I need to be inside her like a bear needs his first meal after winter, but I force myself to push in slowly, knowing I'm big, and she's a little pixie.

She arches, her head dropping back as she thrusts her hips up to take me deeper.

Blyad'. She needs more? I'll give it to her. I cage her throat with my hand. I don't squeeze at all—not even a little bit, but the position itself is dominant. I hold her throat and shove my cock in with a hard thrust.

"Oh my *gawd.*" Story's mouth opens wide, her body undulating beneath mine, responding to my thrust.

I ease back then arc in again with force, keeping her from sliding up with the hand around her throat. Her core contracts around my cock. With my free hand, I pinch her nipple then squeeze her perfect breast.

I go slow and hard for a while, punctuating my in-strokes with a pause to let her feel my full length, to get used to me. But both of us soon need more. Story starts reaching for me, holding my sides to pull me in sooner, so I shorten the strokes and increase the pace, leaning one hand against the wall behind her head to brace myself.

"Oleg," she pants. "Oh my God, yes. Oleg."

Hearing her chant my name sends my ego on a victory march before it's even over. The most human part of me that had shriveled up and died turning on a little more each time I drink in her goddess-beautiful face.

Story. I want to chant her name back to her. My *lastochka.* I shift to lift her legs up to my shoulders, holding the fronts of her thighs, so I can plow deeper. Her cries get louder and more frequent—almost a constant stream of vocalizations.

I pause and arch a brow. *You like that,* shalun'ya?

Spank me, Daddy. Remembering her squeal when I put her over my shoulder Saturday night, I pull out and flip her to belly, giving each buttcheek a sharp slap.

"Ooh!" She arches her back like a cat, offering her ass up to me. I deliver another two slaps before I push back in, and she moans her contentment.

I hold her by the nape and ride her from behind, glorying in each delicious, dizzying stroke. The room swoops and swims, but it's from ecstasy not pain. Nothing feels so right as being inside Story.

I stroke down her back with the fingertips of my free hand. Admire the umbrella tattoo on her shoulder blade. Grab a handful of her ass. Hold her hip. I pull her cheeks wide to get at her cute little hole, and she lets out a stream of frantic, garbled encouragement. She doesn't last long. Four more stokes, and then she comes, her legs straightening and jerking, her inner walls squeezing my cock like a fist.

I fuck her harder and faster to bring on my own finish, and it comes immediately. I plunge deep and hold, reaching my hand under her hips to rub her clit and coax out the rest of her climax. It works. Another gigantic tremor runs through her, and the muscles pulse again, squeezing more cum into the condom. Sparks of light dance behind my eyes. I pull out and topple to my side, my head splitting but my heart, my spirit—something I thought long dead—soaring like a fucking kite.

Story, I want to croon in her ear. Beautiful story. My crazy, wild, naughty girl songbird. What a fucking priviledge to be in her bed. I settle for a soft hum. The sound for how she makes me feel.

I manage to remove the condom and throw it in the trash by the bed before I close my eyes and pass out again.

~

STORY

I'm just out of the shower getting dressed when a knock sounds on the door. Oleg is passed out on the bed, poor guy.

Poor him, lucky me. The guy is a freaking stallion. That was by far the best sex I've ever had. It wasn't any special technique, it was just... Oleg. I love feeling his strength and power. The roughness and dominance to his movements. And yet I've also never felt so safe with a guy. This guy is dependable. He comes to every show. Sits in the front with the energy of a bouncer or protector. I never once felt nervous when he was manhandling me. I knew if I said stop, he'd stop. I could relax and enjoy it.

I yank on my sweater run for the door. No one rang the buzzer downstairs, which means it must be a neighbor. Hopefully not to complain about our morning sex session. Not that I was *that* loud. Or was I? My throat does feel rather raw.

I swing the door open, but when I see the two tattooed guys behind it, I immediately narrow the gap until only my face shows through. "Yes?"

"Hey, Story," the brown-haired guy says. "I'm Maxim, a friend of Oleg's. This is Pavel." He indicates his blond friend. "We met at your show? My wife Sasha talked to you—the redhead?"

"Yeah, hey." I remember the guy and his friendly wife, and he doesn't seem threatening, but I don't know who hurt Oleg, and the guy smashed his own phone like he was afraid of being tracked. Plus, I don't know how these guys found me or my place.

"I'm sorry to show up here. It's just that we haven't seen Oleg since Saturday night, and we were wondering if you know anything? Was he at your show Saturday?"

I shake my head quickly. "No."

He cocks his head like he knows I'm lying.

"I mean, yes, he was at my show, but I don't know where he went after that. I mean, I haven't seen him." Damn, I'm a terrible liar. I sound breathless, and I'm speaking way too fast.

Maxim's eyes narrow. He tries to peer past me, and when he does, his shoulders relax. "Oleg, what the fuck?"

I whirl to find Oleg behind me. He pulled on his jeans, but he's shirtless, and there are no shoes on his feet. He's certainly not hiding from these guys. Relief flows through me.

I'm suddenly overjoyed to have someone to share the weight of Oleg's plight with. "He got attacked. Someone shot him," I blurt, standing back from the door, so they can come in.

"What?" Maxim scans Oleg quickly.

"He got hit over the head and shot in the leg." I point at the hole in his jeans. I washed the blood out, but the entire thigh area of his jeans is still stained rust.

"Fuck." Maxim says something terse in Russian to Pavel who appears grim. "Thank you for taking care of him."

"You don't have to thank me." I'm slightly offended. Of course, I took care of him. He's my friend.

Oleg staggers back toward the bedroom, and Pavel follows him, not offering help but staying close.

"Do you know who attacked him? Did you see what happened?"

I shake my head. "No, he drove my van here to take me home. The next morning, I found him in the back of it, bleeding with a wound on the back of his head."

Oleg appears with his shirt and boots on.

"Where the fuck is your phone?" Maxim demands. I bristle a little at the way he speaks to Oleg, but it also puts me at ease. They're obviously comfortable with each other. There's a rapport. Like I have with Flynn and the guys in the band.

Oleg doesn't answer. Well, of course not, but he doesn't try to communicate at all. I've noticed him do that with me, too, when he decides he doesn't want to engage. It's like he doesn't even try.

"He smashed it," I offer, even though I'm not sure Oleg wants me to share that.

Maxim stares at him, like he's trying to puzzle it out. "Okay," he says, like he's got it handled. "Let's get you home, buddy."

Oleg looks at Maxim and tips his head my way.

Maxim pulls out his wallet and grabs all the cash in it. I catch sight of more than a few hundred dollar bills. He folds the wad in half and hands it all to me, pinched between his index and middle fingers. "Thank you for taking care of Oleg."

"What?" I shove the bills back at him, offended. "I didn't do it for the money."

Oleg appears alarmed by my tone. His brows go up, and he watches my face carefully.

"No, no, no," Maxim says smoothly. "I didn't mean it to sound transactional." He spreads his free hand in a peace-making gesture. "Not at all. I know you did it because you care about Oleg."

I calm down a bit.

"But Oleg wants you to be taken care of. Please accept it." He stretches his arm out toward me again.

I hesitate. I'm still a little offended. Or maybe I don't like that Oleg's leaving. He's leaving, and I don't have his number or know when I'm going to see him again.

This is so unlike me. Usually I'm the one running from a relationship.

My eyes suddenly get hot, and I blink rapidly. I still haven't taken the money. I sort of hate that I'm talking to Maxim right now instead of Oleg.

Why is that?

Why is Oleg letting his friend speak for him? And why is he just leaving with them? Is he even going to say goodbye?

It pisses me off. I fold my arms across my chest. "Then let Oleg give it to me," I challenge.

Maxim pivots, so his arm points toward Oleg. Oleg's dark brows are down. He snatches the money from Maxim's fingers and tosses it on my coffee table like he's throwing it in the trash. He steps right into my space, cupping the back of my head, his mouth descending on mine before I even have time to breathe. To think.

The tears spear the inner corners of my eyes as I receive his kiss. His hand on my waist, his thumb cupping my cheek. When he breaks the kiss, he leans his forehead against mine and stays there. He makes that soft humming sound he did after we had sex. His friends leave the apartment, standing out on the landing to give us privacy.

"Don't do that to me," I whisper, hurt still lacing my voice.

He pulls away, worried eyes studying my face.

"I don't want an intermediary between us," I explain because he obviously isn't sure what I'm talking about.

He goes still, almost like I shocked him. Like he wasn't

aware of the way he just faded into the background the moment his friends arrived. He nods and bends his head to give me one soft kiss—a press of his lips to mine.

I don't want him to leave. It's crazy how much I don't want him to leave. Even though I know this thing can't go anywhere. I know exploring it will only lead to pain and the eventual end. Still, I cling to him. Wrap my arms around his back and press my body up against his in a hug.

"Get better soon," I say, my voice rusty. It's a stupid thing to say. It doesn't encompass one-fifth of what I want to say to him. "Will you be at my show?"

Jesus.

Now I just sound clingy.

He freezes again, which tells me he doesn't think he will be, but then he gives a single nod.

Hmm. I don't quite believe him.

But there's someone after him. Maybe he has to go into hiding now.

Fuck—maybe I'll never see him again.

I catch his sleeve as he turns. "Oleg—"

He swivels back, that alarmed expression in place.

"Will you be? Really?"

He draws in a slow breath then nods.

I exhale.

"Be careful," I say because now I feel guilty for asking him to come to my show when he's obviously in danger.

He nods and catches my hand, squeezing it.

I still don't want him to go. But his friends shift position in the hallway, and I notice the bulge of a handgun in Pavel's jacket pocket, and I remember that I don't belong in his world. Which means he can't stay in mine.

"Bye," I say quickly, turning away to pretend I'm cool. Because I am. I've had a lot of weird experiences in my short life. I'm in a band, and many of my friends do a lot of drugs. This will become another crazy story. Or maybe I'll actually write the songs that have been eluding me for a while now.

Why, then, does it feel like such a loss when Oleg walks out my door?

CHAPTER 4

Oleg

I climb in the back of Maxim's Tesla.

"Give him your phone," Maxim barks and Pavel.

Pavel hands me his phone, and Maxim hands his to Pavel as he puts the car in drive and pulls out.

"Who was it?" Maxim demands.

My head throbs, and I still feel raw and rough from upsetting Story back there. Fuck. I definitely didn't mean to offend her by having Maxim give her money. I just expected him to do and say the right things because I can't say them myself. I wanted to take care of her. And I'm sure she could use the money. I did the math in my head. She can't bring in more than eight hundred a week giving guitar lessons. So it's not terrible money, but it's not like she's rich or anything. And Maxim is. He was smooth as fuck, too—saying all the right things, and it still pissed her off.

She didn't want him talking for me.

I'm still rocked to the core by that. Like torn down the center of the chest, heart exposed where it beats. I've never felt so vulnerable in my life.

And I still don't know what I'm going to tell Ravil and the guys about this. I want to ignore Maxim, but I know that's not going to fly, so I type in the details in Russian.

Three guys. Spoke Russian. I fought them and got away. I don't tell him that they wanted me alive.

That I know why.

Pavel reads my brief text out loud for Maxim. For me, it's not brief. It's about the longest I usually get with any communique.

"It's the three guys Dima tracked into the country." Maxim smacks the dash. "Call Dima and tell him to text the photos to my phone."

I remember now that Maxim had Dima set up tracking software to flag any persons of interest from all incoming Russian flights because he feared someone from the Moscow bratva would try to kill Sasha for her millions. If those meatheads who tried to capture me Saturday came over recently, Dima would've noted it. They weren't bratva, but they still might've raised flags.

Pavel makes the call, and a few moments later Ravil's phone buzzes with the incoming texts. I open them, then nod at Pavel. Maxim catches it in the rearview mirror.

"Fuck!" Maxim explodes. "I knew they were trouble. Did they ask anything? Say anything?"

I shake my throbbing head. My pulse races. Maxim believes this is about Sasha. I shouldn't let him. I should come clean about my past.

But then, I should've done that two years ago when Ravil brought me into the fold. I can't do it now without them all feeling my betrayal.

"Did all three walk away?" Pavel asks. Which really means, *did I do any real harm to them?* Sadly, no.

I shrug and nod.

And thankfully, that ends my interrogation. The guys are so used to me offering nothing that they don't push. Maxim heard what he needed to hear. He will guard his bride and put systems in place to locate these guys. To eliminate the threat.

Which works in my favor, of course. Until whoever is after me sends another crew.

Maxim's phone rings, and Dima's name comes on the screen. Dima is our hacker. There's nothing the guy can't hack or program.

I hand the phone back to Maxim since I obviously can't answer. "Those were the guys," Maxim confirms.

"I have a location," Dima clips, all business. Ravil's organization is smooth and orderly—efficient. Pavel was in the Russian military. Ravil and Maxim are genius-level strategists. Nikolai, Dima's twin, is a bookie. I'm the muscle. The enforcer. But we're a team—the spokes of a wheel.

"Text it to me." Maxim twists around to look at me. "You okay with a detour? You don't have to come in."

I'm not. I will need to hurl as soon as the Denali stops, and I'm pretty desperate for a painkiller, but of course, I nod. Killing these fuckers is top priority. How I'm feeling is totally irrelevant.

Maxim navigates through traffic. I open the door at a red light to puke, and he curses in Russian.

"Maybe we should take him back first," Pavel says. His gun is on his lap, silencer already screwed on.

I pull my head back in the vehicle and slam the door then wave my hand impatiently with a frown.

Pavel shrugs. "Okay. He wants to go."

It's not a long drive. We get to a hotel, and Maxim parks. He twists to look at me, screwing a silencer on his own piece. "We'll be back in ten, okay, O?"

I nod.

"I'll make them pay for what they did to you."

I don't answer. I don't really give a shit if they suffer or don't. They were just doing a job. My real concern is who's behind them.

The guys are back in seven minutes. Maxim checks the mirror and cleans a few splatters of blood from his face before stowing the piece under the seat and taking off.

Pavel sits quietly for a few minutes before he asks, "Don't you think we should've found out who sent them before we killed them?"

A muscle ticks in Maxim's face. He's crazy-protective when it comes to Sasha. It affected his decision-making on this one. "They were waiting for us. If we hadn't fired first, we'd be dead now. Besides, we're sending a fucking message. Anyone who comes near my wife will meet a swift death."

Pavel shoots me a glance to see if I'm with him on this one.

Of course, I'm thankful they didn't get anything out of them. If they had, I might find one of those guns pointing at my head now, so I just shrug.

It worked for me. I needed those assholes out of the picture and away from Story.

The rest of the shit, I can deal with later.

I tune my electric guitar then run through chord changes in fast succession to warm my fingers up. It's Friday afternoon, and the Storytellers are at the Lounge for weekly practice. If it wasn't for Rue letting us practice here during the days for free, there would be no Storytellers. Which is why

Rue's Lounge will always be our home base. People ask me sometimes why we don't try to branch out—get gigs at other places, rotate where we play.

We could. We might even make more money. Maybe we'd build a bigger following. But Rue's launched us. We grew our base of support here. We're as loyal to the owner as she is to us.

"Where's the set list?" Flynn asks me.

People think it's my band because of the name, but it's actually Flynn's. Flynn and his friends got together after high school, formed a band, and then needed a lead singer. They thought a female would make them way cooler than an all-boy band. Of course, my name fit easily for a band name.

Maybe it is my band. I mean, I'm the older sister and creative lead. But I don't ever think of it that way. I believe strongly in collaboration. That's where the magic happens. With the Storytellers, I often feel like I'm just along for the ride.

"So what happened with Silent Boris Saturday night?" Flynn asks.

I whip my head around and glare at him, uncharacteristically on edge. "Don't call him that."

"Seriously, dude. That guy looks like he could kill a man with his bare hands and not break a sweat," Lake says.

"I kind of think he has," Ty agrees. "If I hadn't seen the way he looks at Story, I would be scared to death of him."

Flynn's watching me, though. His mouth stretches into a wide grin. "So you finally sealed the deal with your Russian bodyguard, huh?" He has that sing-song congratulatory tone that makes me bristle even more.

"Shut up. Don't be an idiot." Now I really don't sound like myself. Dang it.

The guys all gawk at me with interest. It's not like me to

get worked up over things. I'm as flighty, follow the energy, and laid back as they come. But the past four days since Oleg's friends came and collected him have been torture. Endlessly long. Filled with questions. Empty. I've worried about Oleg. But more than that, having Oleg at my place changed something in me.

I missed him. Crave more time with him.

All of those things are so unlike me.

Which makes me desperately want to go back to the way things were before. To floating through life without giving two fucks about anything. Especially not a guy.

"Wait." Flynn suddenly sobers, studying me with concern. "Did something bad happen?"

Now the asshole asks. It's a fine time to suddenly be concerned about my well-being, when he's the guy who left with two girls and told me to get Oleg to drive.

"No!" I throw my guitar pick at him.

He dodges it, his pirate grin stretching across his face. "Oh my God… you really like this guy!"

"No," I scoff. I'm definitely not doing *that*. Not the relationship boomerang our mom subjected us to as kids. Falling in love. Breaking up. Grieving. Plunging into depression. Checking herself into mental institutions. It was an endless cycle of full and broken hearts. She and my dad separated and got back together nine times when I was little. When she finally divorced him because he was a cheating bastard, we thought things would calm down, but they didn't. She recreated the same drama with a string of new men.

I'm not like her. I'm the opposite. I hang out with a guy. We hook up. Things get weird. I experience this inner nudge, this restlessness that tells me to cut things off before they go any further.

Flynn is a total man-whore. I'm not like that. I'm not just

out for sex. I do crave real connection. I need to like the guy, to feel the spark, to find him entertaining and smart. But I don't know, after a few months, I get itchy and feel penned in. I always find something that makes me want to end it.

Dahlia, our baby sister, is the only one of the three of us who seems to know how to be in a lasting relationship. She and her high school boyfriend went to college together in Wisconsin and are still going strong.

"Wait, so did something happen?" Flynn just won't let it die. I seriously want to shove my boot up his butt right now.

All three of my bandmates stare at me expectantly. They're not going to let me dodge this question.

"Yes!"

They all grin at me like goofballs.

"And?" Lake prompts. I'm pretty sure he and Ty have always wanted to hook up with me but know that I have no interest and also that Flynn would kick their asses all the way to Tokyo.

"Why are you guys being such *girls* right now?" I demand. "Since when do I share my sex life with you?"

"We're being guys. This is locker room talk. You're the one who hangs with guys, Story," Flynn reminds me.

It's true. Just by default of the amount of time spent together, these guys have become my best friends.

I really need to get out more.

And that thought instantly produces more thoughts of Oleg. Because he's the one who changed up my rhythm. Threw me off my game. He left a sense of emptiness and longing in his wake that I'm having a hard time recovering from.

I did start to write a song, though. A hot, push me up against the wall kind of song. But I'm not ready to reveal it yet.

RENEE ROSE

"It was hot," I admit.

"No shit." Ty tries to sound casual, but there's a warble in his voice like he's disappointed to hear it.

"Blister in the Sun," I say to put the topic to bed and start rehearsal. I pick the start of the Violent Femmes song on my guitar.

"Hang on." Ty scrambles for his drum sticks, almost missing the cue.

And then we're into it. The music. The thing we all adore. It's our addiction and our lives.

I don't know why suddenly it doesn't feel like enough.

CHAPTER 5

S *tory*

He didn't come.

I scan the Saturday night crowd for the eighth time, looking for my big Russian.

He's not here. I can't believe it.

"How are you all doing tonight?" I ask the crowd, faking my enthusiasm to be with them.

There's already a decent crowd of our regulars here, and they cheer their welcome with over-enthusiastic vigor. "Story! We love you!"

I chuckle into the mic. "I love you, too."

I don't feel like playing the set list I put together. At Rue's, we usually play a mix of covers and original pieces. We have enough of our own songs to do an all-original show, and we do when we get booked other places, but playing at the same place every Saturday, it gets old. People like to hear covers mixed in. They get excited about them.

My fingers play a few notes on my electric guitar.

Flynn laughs softly into his mic. He recognizes the song before I even do.

Fuck. It's "Paint it Black" by the Rolling Stones.

I'm not that disappointed by Oleg's absence. But the song choice says differently. I shrug and go for it even though the rest of the band won't know what the hell we're doing. The two of us grew up filling in with our father's classic rock cover band. It's why we have a huge repertoire to pull from.

Ty and Lake get on board fast enough as I take them through my version of the song, which makes our growing audience go wild—possibly because they can tell we're figuring it out as we go along. People like to be a part of the show. Feel like they know you. Like we're friends.

I stop myself from glancing at the table where Oleg should be. The one taken by a group of regulars I recognize.

I somehow knew when he left that he wouldn't be here tonight, and yet his absence pierces me through the gut. He probably is still recovering. He's too dizzy to drive. His head hurts too much for the loud music.

I know all those things, and they are perfectly reasonable explanations for his absence, but my emotions are haywire. They are not perfectly reasonable at all.

I've been raw and needy since he left. Worried for him. And now that I find he's not here—the outcome I was sure I would face—I feel abandoned. This is exactly why I don't like to rely on people. My parents taught me this lesson very well. They loved me, but they had their own demons. Showing up in the way I needed them to just wasn't in the cards.

But Oleg... he was dependable. Like clockwork, every Saturday.

He told me he'd be here.

I know he couldn't call. His phone is still in pieces in my bathroom trash. And he never asked for my number.

But that bothers me, too. He could've tried. Of course, he

doesn't type in English. I forgot that. Ugh! The fact that I'm using all this brainspace on this when I'm in the middle of my performance pisses me off.

I switch back to the planned playlist, and we get through the first set flawlessly. It all feels flat to me, but the audience doesn't seem to notice. If anything, they are more boisterous than usual. There's a festive, party-like atmosphere in the place, and yet I have an uneasy feeling, like I'm being watched. Not the pleasant Oleg's watching feeling. Something more sinister. I scan the place and spot a guy with a scruffy beard and leather bomber jacket standing in the corner who doesn't look like he belongs. He's not smiling or talking to anyone. And he's staring right at me in a creepy way. He's the kind of guy I would never let in my apartment for a guitar lesson.

I find myself wishing Oleg was here to play my fake boyfriend again.

Real boyfriend, a little voice in my head murmurs, but I resist that notion. Because real boyfriends don't last, and I want Oleg to stick around.

Rue waves me over from behind the bar as I walk off the stage to take a break. I met the mohawked owner through a mutual friend back when the Storytellers were just getting going. She invited us to play. Everyone had fun, so she invited us to play again. Pretty soon we were a monthly gig, then weekly. Rue's transformed with us—our crowd became their crowd and vice versa.

It's a hip, eclectic crowd, equal parts hetero and gay, lots of good will, a smattering of drugs. On Friday nights, they have a burlesque show that has also become its own special animal.

I squeeze through the crowd to her, accepting congratulations and greeting as I go until I get to the bar and a regular slides off his stool to offer it to me. "You sit. I was going to get up anyway," he tells me.

Rue hands me a water bottle. "You guys are on fire tonight."

"Are we?" It didn't feel like it. Isn't that always the way it goes. The times I try hardest are the times the audience just stares at me. Or worse—ignores me. But the nights I go on automatic, everyone loves us.

"Where's your biggest fan?" Rue lifts her chin toward Oleg's usual table. "That huge, silent guy who looks at you like he wants to eat you for dinner?"

I find myself looking toward the door, like Oleg might show up any moment. "I don't know where he is." I'm obviously not going to explain that my biggest fan is probably in the Russian mafia and got shot outside my apartment last week.

It's funny how none of that churns my stomach so much as my need to see him again. It's almost like my body aches to be in his physical presence. I want to sit on his lap. Feel the slap of his hand on my ass. The weight and hardness of that big, strong body against mine again.

And the fact that he didn't come? Proves that having sex with him was a mistake.

Oleg was supposed to be the dependable thing in my life. The guy who always shows up like clockwork. The only constant in my chaotic universe.

But now we had sex, and its over. The constant became inconstant.

Rue moves back to making drinks, and I sit, deflecting the conversations people try to start around me.

I sit so long Flynn comes to collect me for our next set— which is odd because I'm usually the one chasing the guys down to get back on stage.

I get up on stage, casting a baleful last glance toward the door and start the last set.

～

Oleg

Closing time. I can't fucking believe it. I haven't missed more than one Saturday night show at Rue's in nine months, and that was to go to Maxim and Sasha's destination wedding.

I sit in the parking lot and watch the back door. The band's van is parked out back, and so is Story's Smart Car, so I know they're still inside. I'll just wait until I see her get safely in her car.

I spent most of the week in bed, recovering. And tonight... I just fucking overslept. I laid down to rest my aching head this afternoon, never dreaming I wouldn't be up and ready to head to Story's show on time. I didn't set an alarm because I didn't think I'd need one. I'd sooner puncture a lung than miss a show.

But when I woke up drenched in sweat with a foggy, aching head, it was already midnight. I had to scramble to take a quick shower and drive down here. I shouldn't be here. I have no idea who's sending men after me or how they tracked me down the first time. I should leave before I put my *lastochka* in danger. But she seemed like she really wanted me here, and the thought of letting her down kills me.

I blink, trying to get my thoughts straight.

Story comes out alone. Her shoulders are hunched, and she walks quickly toward her car. It's unlike her—she's usually surrounded by friends and hangers-on. Guys and girls who want to fuck her. Friends who think she's cool. People who want her at their after-parties to make them happen.

Tonight there's no smile on her face. No cocoon of a crowd.

Dammit. I *did* let her down.

As if she senses me, her head turns, and she looks right through my windshield. There's an accusation in her gaze. Like she's pissed I didn't come. That thought blows through me, straightening my spine, puffing up my chest.

I'm out of the Denali before I even think, but things immediately go sideways.

A guy in a bomber jacket with a beard that needs trimming emerges from the shadowy corner behind her. "Get in the car or your girlfriend's dead." The Russian words are for me. The gun is at Story's head. I put my hands slowly in the air. Look around. A car speeds up and stops between me and the *mudak* with Story.

I see one guy driving, another in the passenger seat. I slowly open the back door of the car. Not because I'm getting in, but to check to see how many guys I have to kill.

It's empty. Easy. I just have to wait until that gun moves away from Story's head. I'm not taking any chances where she's concerned.

I'll wait until we're in the car to kill them both.

Except the asshole seems to know what's important to me because he grabs Story by the arm and brings her to the car. "Get in," he barks in heavily-accented English. He doesn't move to open the door for her.

She looks at me with panic in her eyes, and I try to project calm. I won't let them take her. No fucking way. I will sacrifice myself in a heartbeat before I let anyone touch a hair on her head.

Of course, that's what they're banking on. I'm sure the plan is to torture Story to make me sing. Spill the identity of every client Skal'pel' cut into.

Fuck! How could I let her get involved in this shit?

Story pulls the handle. I palm my gun, keeping it hidden behind my back. Our eyes meet through the back seat of the car.

I just need the right moment.

A distraction. The gun pointed away from Story.

My beautiful, brave swallow reads my mind. She rams her guitar case into her captor's belly. I take the shot across the back seat, then shoot the guy in the front passenger seat.

I have the driver's throat in my hand. I snap his neck.

I shut the back door and wipe my prints from the handle. Running around to the other side, I shove Story's captor's body in the back seat, shut the door and wipe those prints, too.

Story's backed up, shock still frozen on her face. Her eyes are twice the size they usually are.

Fuck!

I point to my Denali, praying she won't run from me, but to my relief, she dashes to the Denali and climbs in. She still trusts me. Even after what she just saw.

I roll down the window on the driver's side, put the car in drive and shove the driver's foot over to the gas. Then I steer through the window to get the car out of Rue's parking lot. When I get it into the alley, I point it down the street, jogging with it for a half a block until I'm sure it will keep going straight onto a major road.

I whip around to see headlights behind me, but they're my own Denali, Story behind the wheel.

That's my girl.

I run for it, throwing open the driver's door as she climbs into the passenger side, acrobatic as ever.

I've never felt the need to speak more. I reach over and take Story's hand at the same time I take off out of there, driving backward down the alley with my lights off until I'm out of the neighborhood.

The fact that she hasn't spoken scares the shit out of me. I'm sure she's in shock. I can't say how fucking grateful I am that she got in my Denali of her own volition.

Because if she hadn't, I would've had to force her. Story is no longer safe. That much is clear. Because I don't know if I eliminated the real threat tonight or just another hired gang.

Story's eyes are wide, and her breath rasps in and out, but she's craning her neck, looking over her shoulder. She hasn't shut down completely.

I want to tell her it's okay.

I won't let anyone hurt her.

I need her to come with me to lie low for a while.

I want to say I'm sorry. So fucking sorry. Nothing surpasses my anguish at having put her in danger this way. I made her a target. It's unforgivable.

"Where are we going?" she asks once.

I reply with what I hope is a reassuring squeeze of her hand. Her phone rings, but she doesn't answer it.

I drive straight to my place in Ravil's building—what the neighbors have dubbed "the Kremlin" because the entire building is filled with Russians. When I park and turn off the car, Story turns to me. Her face is pale and serious.

"Are you going to tell me what's going on?"

Fuck.

I get out and walk around to open her door, but she's already hopped out, her guitar strap looped over her shoulder.

I cup her face and peer down into it, stroking her cheeks with my thumbs.

She nods. "I'm okay."

Fuck. Her mind-reading thing only makes me twenty thousand times more addicted to her.

I draw in a relieved breath and nod back. I take her hand and lead her to the bank of elevators, swiping my card that gets me to the top floor. The penthouse suite Ravil shares with his cell.

Since he had a baby boy in November, I keep waiting for Ravil to kick us all out—to move us to a different floor, so he can use the penthouse for his new family. But apparently, his new wife Lucy doesn't mind.

The other newlyweds—Maxim and Sasha don't seem to mind communal living either. Which, frankly, is all the better for me. It's harder to disappear in a smaller group, and disappearing is definitely my game.

My suite has its own entrance from the elevator hallway, which is good because it's late. Even if it weren't, I wouldn't subject Story to the chaos of the group right now.

I think the private entrance is supposed to make up for the fact that I don't have a view of the lake, not that it matters to me. My floor-to-ceiling windows look out over the city.

I swipe my keycard through the lock and push the door open. The shades are drawn, and the suite is dark.

Story steps in, and I flick on a lamp, so she can see. Everything in the penthouse is expensive and tasteful, but the decorator Ravil hired got the message that I wasn't interested in anything fancy, so she left it mostly empty. There's a minimalist king platform bed, low to the ground, and a large overstuffed chair. The end tables and dresser are mid-century modern teak. There's a small table with two chairs in front of the window. It's probably all expensive—I don't know. I don't care about any of it. It's a place to sleep—that's all that matters to me.

"This is your place?" She looks up at me.

I nod.

She still seems shaken and stiff. I can't stand it. I would

do fucking anything to erase what just happened back there. What she saw me do.

Fuck!

She sets down her acoustic guitar and takes off her wine-colored woolen coat, draping it over the neck of the case. "Where's the kitchen?"

I lift my brows and mime eating.

"No, I'm not hungry. I just think it's weird that you don't have one."

I nod. I don't know how to begin explaining that I live with seven and a half other people—six Russians, one American, and a baby named Benjamin.

She kicks off her combat boots and heads into the bathroom. She's in a corduroy micro-mini, frayed at the edges, with a pair of pale pink tights on underneath. On top, she's wearing a skin-tight t-shirt with a rainbow across her chest and the sleeves cut off. I think it might have belonged to a child before it became Story's.

"Wow. This is...beautiful." She opens the shower door and takes in the giant shower. She turns on the water and looks over her shoulder at me. "Looks like there's room for two."

It's not flirty, she almost sounds... vulnerable.

She needs me. It's my job to take care of her. I follow her in, stripping off my clothes as I walk. She drops her skirt to the floor at her feet and shimmies out of the tights. I tug the t-shirt off over her head and unhook her bra. I don't feel the aggression I felt last time. The wild storm of lust that made me rough and crude with her. This time, the need to take care of her is too strong.

She just saw me kill three men. She saw that, and she's still here with me. She didn't protest me bringing her here, and she hasn't tried to leave.

She asked me into the shower with her.

But she's not okay. I know that in my bones, and my need to soothe her comes first.

I know I'm right, when she just turns and steps into the shower. It's like she wants to wash off the events of the night. I finish undressing and step in behind her, shutting the door.

I don't crowd her, but she comes to me, her fingers coasting over my hairy chest.

"Why didn't you come tonight?" she asks.

I flinch, the question hitting me like a punch to the gut. I'd tried to tell myself I didn't matter enough to Story. That she wouldn't be hurt by my absence tonight, but she clearly was. I trail my fingertips down her face, tracing the water droplets over her nose, then her lips.

"Was it because of those guys?"

Fuck. I don't want to tell her it was because I overslept. And of course, I don't have a way of giving her the words, even if I had them. I step into her space, walking her slowly backward until she hits the soft quartz wall. My hands coast lightly down her arms. One settles on her waist, the other wraps behind her neck. I lean my forehead against hers.

"You're sorry," she murmurs, doing her trick of reading my mind.

I nod.

When she looks up, there are tears in her eyes. "I'm scared, Oleg." She sucks in a sobbed breath. "I don't know what's happening, and you can't tell me."

I wrap my arms around her, and she presses her cheek to my chest, crying. I hold her until her tears subside. It doesn't take long. She sniffs and pushes me gently back. I pick up the bar of soap and roll it in one hand, then gently begin to suds down one of her arms to her hands, where I massage each calloused fingertip. I turn her and wash her back, massaging her neck firmly, stroking down her sides, gripping her ass possessively.

She moans softly. "Yes."

I soap the other shoulder and arm, then both her breasts, pressing my thigh between her legs and pinning her against the shower wall. I tug her head back with my hand around her wet hair. She opens her mouth. Our lips connect for a searing kiss then come apart.

"I'm on the pill," she murmurs.

I check her face to be sure I'm getting the right memo.

"Are you clean?"

I nod. Definitely clean. I've only had sex twice since I got out of prison, and both times I wore a condom.

"Me too." She reaches for my cock.

I wasn't going to go there unless I was sure she needed it, but apparently she does.

I impale her with my erection in one swift stroke. Being inside her bare is another incredible level. But this isn't for me. It's for her. I need to give my *lastochka* what she needs.

She gasps, lifting one leg to wrap around my waist, clinging to my shoulders for stability. I fill her, pumping in and out, her skin under my hands a form of worship.

Her breath rasps. Her gaze stays on my face, intensifying the moment. She's searching for something. Connection? Truth? Trust?

I wish I fucking knew how to give it to her. All I know is our bodies, so right together. Our skin, wet and slick. The communion of this act, this coming together for mutual release. I know I need this as badly as she does, even though I'd willingly deny myself the pleasure if it meant I could undo what happened tonight.

I work her ass in my hands, massaging it, stroking between her cheeks. Pressing against her anus.

Her eyes fly open in surprise, and her hips thrust frantically, taking me deeper, meeting my strokes.

You like that? You want my finger in your ass while I make you come?

That's what I would say if I could just dirty-talk my girl.

I bend my neck to meld my lips to hers, drinking in her gasps as I work my fingertip into her anus. When her head arcs back, I kiss her throat and gently pump my finger in and out, just to the first knuckle as I hold her hips captive and thrust into her.

She shatters—throwing herself fully in my arms, both legs wrapped tightly around my waist as she comes. Her nails score my neck and shoulders, the contracting of her muscles around my dick bringing on my own release. I stay deep but rub her clit up and down over my loins, my erection straining with each mini-thrust. I come inside her, and she squeezes more, milking my dick for its seed. I fucking love that I can feel everything. That I'm inside her without any barriers between us.

"Oleg." She sounds broken.

I don't put her down. I don't ever want to put her down again. I ease my finger out of her ass and wash us both under the water, then carry her out of the shower, still wrapped around my waist. I grab a towel and pull it tightly around her back and ass, using it to hold her against my body. Carefully, like she's made of glass, I prop her ass on the bathroom counter, the towel tucked softly beneath her cheeks, and I use the ends to pat her face dry. Her make-up left smudges under her eyes, but I don't know what to do about those. We'll figure it out in the morning.

I run the corner of the towel between her breasts and down her belly, wrap both sides up to dry her thighs, and then

I pull her back into my arms, wrap the towel around her back and carry her to my bed.

Story's quiet the whole time, watching me with big, brown eyes. I lay her gently down and flick off the light before I lie beside her. The chaotic thudding in my chest is soothed when she instantly rolls into me, molding her body against my side, resting her wet head on my shoulder.

"You're warm," she murmurs.

She's right, I'm burning up. But the only thing I care about is holding Story.

CHAPTER 6

S tory

For a moment, when I wake, I don't recognize where I am. The soft sheets, the warm bed. The sense of comfort. There's a feeling of safety and of the presence of another, but I can't quite remember…

I open my eyes, and it all comes rushing back to me.

Oleg.

It's amazing how comforting his presence is to me. Grounding. Solid. When I'm around him, the chaos in my head seems to quiet.

Oleg is up and dressed, sitting at a table near the curtains. A bag from the local bagel place sits on the table, along with a cup of take-out coffee. The scent gets me out of bed.

I don't want to think about last night.

The gun at my head.

The three men Oleg killed. The trouble he must be in. I know I need to demand answers—we're going to figure out how to communicate one way or another—but part of me isn't sure I even want to know what he's into.

I was a witness to murder last night.

I don't even want to think about all the horrible things that could mean. Right now, without knowing Oleg's story, I can make up my own fairytale around it. He's the innocent one being hunted. He did what he had to do to protect me, the girl he loves, because I got caught in the middle of it.

That's the pretty way I want to spin the story.

This is what I've always done. I live in the area between fantasy and reality. My life has never been structured and organized. I had the opposite of what you could call a "stable home life." There was love—so much love—but it wasn't stable.

But what if it's uglier than that? What if Oleg's the villain in the story?

No.

He's not. I know that from the deepest place in my soul. Not the man who touches me like I'm the most precious thing in the universe. Who looks at me like I'm the only other being in the world. He can't be bad.

Just like my mother isn't bad for all her nervous breakdowns, live-in boyfriends and bad breakups. And my father isn't bad for drinking too much, sleeping with every band groupie who came into his life, and putting his kids last.

I've lived in total chaos my whole life. I think that's why I choose to live alone now. Because my thoughts are messy and disorganized, and usually, when I add someone else to the mix, I lose myself completely. Except that doesn't seem to happen with Oleg. Maybe because he doesn't talk. I don't want to look at that like a plus, but he not only doesn't add to the noise, *he absorbs it.*

Now that I've identified it, I'm sure that's why having him at my shows made it so fabulous for me. He somehow gave me space in the chaos.

"Good morning, sunshine." I kiss his temple.

Oleg's dark gaze sweeps over my naked form and grows hooded.

My nipples pucker at his appreciation.

Purposely provoking him, I dance out of his reach to the wall of curtains, curious to see what's behind them. I yank them back and gasp. "Whoa."

It's an entire wall of floor to ceiling windows looking out over the city. "This is incredible, Oleg." I take another look around the place in the light of day, drinking in what, in the shock of last night's trauma, I failed to notice. This place is gorgeous. And expensive. It's weird because it's just a studio without any kitchen—not even a mini fridge, unless I'm missing something—but it's very high end. We're in some kind of small penthouse on the top of a building that must be very close to Lake Michigan. I'll bet other apartments in the building have lake views.

"Can people see in?" I ask, realizing if they can I'm putting on quite a show.

Oleg makes a popping sound with his lips. I turn to find a t-shirt flying through the air at me.

"Thanks." I catch it and shake it open. It's one of Oleg's shirts—soft cotton and hunter green. It's gigantic. I pull it over my head, and it almost falls to my knees.

"Is this a hotel?"

Oleg shakes his head.

"This is your place?"

A nod.

"I love it." I race past him to leap onto the bed, which, sadly, doesn't bounce. "Except your bed has no springs." I pick up a pillow and lob it at him. "You need a bed with springs, so I can jump on it."

He catches the pillow. The corners of his mouth tick in a barely perceptible smile. I realize I have never—not once—

seen this man smile. His face is usually as inexpressive as his voice, which makes him doubly hard to read.

I've just been going by his intense stares—reading everything into those. Or maybe just his solid presence.

I jump off the bed and go to him, like I'm drawn to a magnet. Now that he's touched me, I can't get enough. I need more of this giant bear-man who's always watching me. I push him down into the chair and climb in his lap, careful to avoid his injury. I guess because he can't give me his words, I crave physical touch with him. Not even sexual—although *holy hell—last night!* But I'd take any contact right now.

Oleg pulls me in, molding his arms around my hips and back to cradle me against him. I lean my head against his giant shoulder, and he shakes open the bagel bag and brings it under my nose.

I shove my hand in the bag and fish for a cinnamon raisin one. Oleg cracks open the cream cheese and hands me a plastic knife.

"Mmm, this is good." I reach for the coffee, opening a tiny container of half and half and dumping it in. "They make these too small, don't you think?"

Of course, he doesn't acknowledge my words. I don't really expect him to. It's okay, I can talk enough for two of us.

"I need, like, five of these for one coffee." I open the other three packets that were on the table and empty them into my cup then try my coffee. Still too black.

Oleg's brow wrinkles, like he's concerned.

I shrug. "I'll live. I'm just grateful for the coffee. You don't drink it?"

"When did you even go to get bagels?" I straighten myself on his lap to spread the cream cheese. I twist to look at him and raise my brows. I swear to God, he's going to have to start *trying* to communicate. I mean, he could gesture. He could draw, like he did at my apartment to let me know to move the van.

This is a problem for me. Oleg doesn't just not speak. It's like he's abandoned all other methods of communication as well.

Maybe no one tries with him. He's been written off. Or he wrote himself off. That thought sends a sharp shard of pain straight through my chest because it rings true, but I steel myself against it.

I know I'm probably nuts. The red flag should've been when he got shot in front of my apartment or when I saw him expertly assassinate three men in about fifteen seconds. But that's not it for me. I don't know, I've already seen and experienced some crazy things in my short life. I've witnessed death before. Not murder, but a drug overdose at a party and a car accident. Oh, and two friends committed suicide when I was in high school. My tolerance for trauma has been built up.

For me, the red flag is this side of Oleg. The stone-faced man who doesn't respond to direct questions. I want the guy who makes his thoughts felt and heard, through his touch, through his energy. The guy I got to know at my apartment before his friends showed up.

I don't know what's going on with him. I don't know who those men were or what they wanted from him. I don't know what Oleg's thinking about at all and what he plans to do. But I do know that Oleg needs to figure out how to explain things to me.

I wish I had a smartphone. We could probably find an app to translate-text to each other, but all I have is my flip phone. I've been stubborn about upgrading—half because I like how much it shocks people that I'm still on the earliest cell phone technology and partly because it's an expense I don't care to incur. My money goes to stuff for the band. I never needed a fancy phone.

I finish my bagel and coffee. "I missed you last night. At my show." I don't say it to make him feel bad. Only because I want him to know. He matters. We may have rarely spoken all those months, but I felt his participation and vitaly and viscerally as I felt the strings under my fingers or the mic in my hand.

His gaze holds regret.

"Where were you?"

His expression closes. Turns blank. It's his non-answering face. Frustration wells in me. I set the guitar back in the case.

"Were you in hiding?"

No answer.

"Why were those guys after you?"

Of course, he can't answer that one, but he's gone dead on me, and it drives me freaking insane. I snap up the locks on my guitar case and slide off the bed. "Listen, you can't do that to me. I know you can't speak, but there are so many other ways to communicate, and you don't even try."

He stares at me, eyes wide. At least I got his expression to change.

I wait, but he still makes no move. No gesture. No attempt.

"Well, I'm not sticking around for this," I say, even though it feels all wrong to leave.

And I'm a chronic leaver.

But this would've happened eventually. I knew that when it started. It's how all my relationships fizzle. This one just exploded rather than fizzled. I'm definitely sorry things went down this way, but I need to cut my losses and go.

Oleg catches my arm. His hand is gentle, but he holds me firmly. I meet his eye. He shakes his head.

"No, what? You gotta give me more."

He points to the door and shakes his head. Okay, he's trying, but that just pisses me off even more. He doesn't get to tell me not to leave when he refuses to even try to communicate otherwise. I shake off his touch. I head into the bathroom to use the toilet and mouthwash. I find my clothes. I pull on the panties, tights, and skirt, which barely shows beneath his long shirt.

Oleg stands in the middle of his beautiful apartment. He watches me, unease in his shoulders.

"Catch you on the flip side." I rise up on my tiptoes and kiss his jaw. A muscle flexes in it. I know he's shaking his head, but I ignore it and head past him to the door where I shove my feet in my boots and pick up my jacket and guitar.

I feel Oleg moving up behind me but don't acknowledge his presence. Not until his giant ham-hand leans against the door to keep me from opening it.

"Oh really." My voice drips with disbelief. "You're going to stop me?" I'm used to Oleg being a gentleman. Holding me captive feels out of character.

His hand doesn't move.

I whirl to face him, chin up. There's regret in his expression. His brows are down, his eyes troubled. He shakes his head.

It occurs to me that the narrative in my head might be a totally different one than his. Is he stopping me because he's trying to protect me or is he keeping me prisoner? A sobering thought occurs to me. Is he worried I'll call the police on him?

"I won't tell anyone about last night. You know that, right?"

He nods without hesitation.

Okay, he does trust me.

"All right. Good. I really need to get home."

He still won't move his hand.

"Oleg." I shove at his chest, which gets me exactly nowhere. "I'm not staying here to be stonewalled by you!"

His eyes widen in surprise. He takes his hand from the door. I seize the moment and grab the handle to yank the door open.

It slams in my face. Oleg gives my ass a single smack like I'm an errant child. It stings and tingles, making heat bloom in my core.

"Oh really? You're going to spank me?" Now, I'm annoyed *and* horny. My panties are already damp. I send a challenging look over my shoulder. "Well, you'd better finish that thought, or I'm just going to be pissed."

His brows shoot up. He moves slowly, like he's making sure he understood me correctly, capturing both my wrists in one of his hands and pinning them to the door. When I don't protest, he smacks my ass with his other hand, harder this time, then squeezes my offended cheek.

I let out a shaky breath, my pussy contracting. He nudges my feet wider. I arch my back and show him I really want it. He pulls the t-shirt off from my head and flattens my palms on the door. Leaving my hands unattended, he loops his forearm around my waist and yanks my panties down my thighs. Then he lights my ass on fire with swift, hard spanks. Like any time Oleg decides to go forward, he doesn't hold back.

I gasp and squeeze my buttcheeks. It's too much but also so good, so thrilling to me, that I bite my lip to keep from protesting.

I squirm under the onslaught. It's right on the line

between pain and pleasure. I hate it and love it at the same time. But when he slides the fingers of his other hand between my legs and palms my pussy while he keeps spanking, I flip *way* over to the side of pleasure. Delirious, erotic pleasure.

"Yeah," I whisper-moan when his fingers start to move between my legs. I arch my back, stick my ass out, grind into his palm. It's incredible.

The best thing ever.

"Ow. Oh…Oleg," I gasp.

So unexpected. I had no idea I'd like this sort of thing.

One of his fingers sinks into me while I continue to ride his palm. I'm dancing under the sharp spanks he's delivering, writhing and bucking. My cheek presses against the door. I don't even recognize the panting needy woman dripping arousal down Oleg's fingers as he spanks me hard until I—

Come.

Oh God, do I come. Hot, quick bursts of pleasure like popcorn explosions go off in my core. I see stars.

I reach my hand back to protect my ass from any further spanks, and Oleg instantly folds it behind my back like I'm his prisoner and massages my punished flesh with rough squeezes. His other hand still works between my legs, fingers slowly plunging in and out as I grind down into the cup of his hand.

Oleg

I slip my fingers out of Story. My lips find her jaw, drag back to her ear, leaving a trail of hot kisses against her smooth skin. I breathe in her sweet, vanilla scent. My *shalun'ya* loved her spanking. Her juices coat my fingers, her pulse beneath my lips still hectic. I wish I'd paid more attention to the discussions in the living room about whipping women.

Ravil met his wife Lucy at some private club in D.C. where he did such a thing to her. And last month, Pavel consensually enslaved a friend of Sasha's after dominating her at the sister club in Los Angeles. He spends his nights demanding her sexual obedience via videoconference every night and flies out there to tie her up and hurt her in person every weekend. That's already more than I wanted to know. I didn't listen to the banter because picturing my roommates having kinky sex isn't how I want to spend my time.

Now, though I wish I knew more nuances. I keep slowly running my middle finger through her plump, slick flesh. Everytime I circle her clit, she comes again—an aftershock that makes her muscles squeeze and lift and her breath catch.

Does she want my cock? What part of this did she like? The pain or dominance? Maybe not the pain because she covered her ass at the end like it was too much. I test my theory and use her wrists behind her back to maneuver her to the bed.

She goes easily. Willingly. Docilely. She wants more.

At least I think so. I sit on the edge of the bed and stand her between my knees. My cock strains to get out of my jeans. I rid her of the panties still tangled around her thighs. Her cheeks are high with color, her eyes glassy.

I tug downward on her hips, and she follows the command, dropping to her knees. She reaches for my cock, but I catch her hands and place them on top of her head, causing her breasts to lift and separate. Her nipples are hard and thick. I lean forward to use my lips on it. I'm able to make light suction with them. I sweep my finger inside my mouth to gather saliva and paint it around her nipple.

She lets out a little moan. "This is… hot." Her voice is rusty. I squeeze her ass and cock my head to the side to ask her to go on. "I like when you go Big Daddy on me. So much." Her head drops back when I move my mouth to the other nipple. "I didn't even know what I was missing. But now…" She licks her lips, making my dick leap against the zipper. She drops her gaze to it and lifts to meet mine again. "I think you may have ruined regular sex for me."

Aw, fuck. I release my erection.

She reaches for it, but once again, I stay her hands, this time bending them behind her back again. I cup the back of her head and guide her gorgeous mouth down to slide over my cock.

I nearly come the minute she takes me. Hot. Wet. Lush. Her mouth is delicious. It's everything I can do not to thrust my very proportionate cock down her delicate throat.

She seems to love her position—being held pseudo-captive by me. Being pretend-forced to give me oral. She bobs her head over my cock enthusiastically, using her tongue to sweep up the underside, to lick around the head. She covers her teeth with her lips and bobs up and down over the head in short, quick movements.

My fingers wrap into her pale champagne blonde hair, tightening with the pleasure.

It kills me that I don't have a tongue to return the favor. If I did, I would never let her suck my cock unless she was sitting on my face. I would always want to make her come first. Come hardest. Loudest.

My sweet *lastochka.*

I want to come, but I'd rather save it all for Story's pleasure, so I stop her, gently tugging her hair back to pull her off me. She licks around her lips, a note of challenge in her eyes.

She definitely still wants more.

Thank fuck. I'm humbled beyond belief that she wants something from me. That she's taking it from me. After what happened last night, and after I just kept her from leaving, she could just as easily be done with me forever. It could've gone a million ways but this one, and I'm endlessly grateful that we're here.

She stands, and I let her, needing her to show me what she needs. She straddles my waist, gripping my cock and guiding me inside her.

I let out a groan. I usually try to stifle all sounds from my mouth because I hate hearing the incoherent syllables, but this one sounds like it should. Like pleasure. Like gratitude.

Story unbuttons my shirt as she slowly rocks her hips, taking me a little deeper each time. When she gets the shirt open, I rip it off and reach behind my neck to pull off my undershirt with one hand.

"Mmm," Story rumbles. "That's hot." Her blue-tipped fingernails scratch through my chest hairs. "I'm so hot for this. For you." She's babbling breathlessly.

I want to hold my breath to make sure I don't miss a single syllable. That I memorize every word.

"You're like a big daddy-bear who spanks and then cuddles. I'm definitely going to be your bad girl."

Blyad'. Her words snap the leash on my control. Keeping my cock buried inside her, I flip her onto her back and start pounding inside her. She undulates her hips enthusiastically, bending her knees up to receive me. I catch her wrists and pin them beside her head, fucking her with more force than I should.

"Oh God," she moans. "You're so big. It's so good."

I change the strokes up to short and fast, jackhammering into her. Her tits bounce. Her eyes roll back in her head. The sight of her expression of ecstasy nearly makes me come, and

I want to make sure I give it to her right, so I pull out and roll her to her belly.

"Oh God, yes," she encourages, spreading her legs wide. Her ass is red from my hand—redder than I expected, but any guilt I might feel is erased when she looks over her shoulder at me.

She wants it.

It's the first time I've really believed there is a God in this world.

The first time I've felt blessed.

I enter her from behind, shuddering with pleasure at the angle.

"Yes, yes, yes," Story chants. "That's so good. Hello G-spot-love."

I arc in and out of her, slapping her cute ass with my loins each time I slam in.

She braces her hands against the wall and arches her ass up for me, making the hottest picture I've ever seen in my life.

I want to tell her how gorgeous she is. How incredibly hot and beautiful and mind-blowing, but I can't. So I settle for fucking her with every bit of passion in my heart. Time slows. Or maybe speeds up. I can't be sure. My mind slips away. My body and Story's join, my spirit and Story's commune.

I offer up everything I have to her—my strength, my dominance, my protection, but with it also comes every weakness—the stains of my sins, my disfigurement, my obsessive need for her. She receives it all. Like the goddess who knows it is all hers to have. To receive and transmute and return. She is love, itself. Or maybe that's me. What I feel for her. I can't tell because it all rolls into one magnificent outpouring of energy.

She comes first, but the moment she does—one squeeze of her muscles—and I come, too. I roar—forgetting to stifle, to censor my noises. I roar and slam home, my cum leaving me in hot ribbons of ecstasy.

I squeeze my eyes closed because the room spins. I forgot about my injuries—far too absorbed with my little minx.

I pull out and roll her over, then push back in for three more delicious strokes. I wring another orgasm out of my little swallow. She holds my gaze as she arches and comes beneath me.

I hum softly. *Ya lyublyu tebya.*

She goes still and blinks at me, almost as if she heard my thoughts.

My *lastochka* reads minds. Or I projected my feelings so clearly I didn't need to speak. I bury my face in her neck, kissing her soft skin down the side, then across her throat. Worshipping my glorious swallow.

It was way too early for *I love you.* And Story is a flighty bird.

Story sucks on her cheek. "Oleg, I don't—" I put a finger to her lips. Of course, she doesn't love me. She barely knows me. It's not something I would've said out loud if I could have.

She wraps her legs around my back to pull my body the rest of the way down onto hers like eye contact was too intense for her. I roll us both to the side to keep from crushing her.

She hides her face against my chest. "I don't really do relationships." Her words are muffled against my skin. Her breath moves the hairs on my chest. "That's why I never asked you to take me home. Relationships always end quickly for me. I don't do the love thing. My mom ruined her life chasing love." She nuzzles her cheek against my chest, almost like a cat would. "And I didn't really want us to end. I like what we had. You coming to my shows. Watching me. Supporting me. I liked it, and I didn't want it to end."

She sounds shaken.

I wrap my arms around her and hold her tight and hum again. *Ya lyublyu tebya.*

I don't mean to project it. I didn't even mean to think it, but it's the truth. I love her. I don't care if she doesn't love me. Even if she won't have me, I will never stop going to her shows.

CHAPTER 7

$\mathcal{S}$ *tory*

I curl into Oleg on the low bed and rub my ass, which still stings from Oleg's large palm.

"You spanked me." There's amusement in my tone. A tinge of wonder. "Is that like… your thing?" I definitely think it's my new thing. "Do you do that with every girl you're with?"

He doesn't answer.

"Dude." I pinch his nipple, and he gently catches my hand. "I asked you a question. Just because you can't speak doesn't mean you don't try to communicate."

He pulls me back in to snuggle closer against his warm chest and shakes his head.

"No? You don't do that with every girl?"

Another shake. His hand slides down to grip my ass possessively. It makes my belly flip with excitement.

"Only me? Am I the first?"

Shrugs and nods. He strokes up and down my thighs, over the place where the buttock meets thigh.

"You were so reserved about making any moves with me

for all those months. You just came and sat and watched. Now I find out you're rough and passionate." I lean up on one elbow to look at his face. He has light scars running beneath the stubble on his face. The guy has been in lots of fights.

"Hey, we need to figure out a way to talk to each other."

He nods and reaches for the bedside table. I see he's written out a list of the Roman alphabet letters with the Cyrillic alphabet symbols beside each one.

"You're learning our alphabet." My heart lurches a bit. "For me?"

His brows come down as he nods, which I interpret to mean, *of course, for you.*

I push up to lean on my hand, sitting up more. "We should learn sign language."

Oleg blinks at me.

"I'll bet they teach it at the community college. We can both learn it. Your friends can learn it, too." I'm pretty excited about my idea although I don't know why I'm making long-term plans with this guy. It scares the hell out of me.

Oleg nods, watching my face like he's afraid I'll disappear if he looks away.

"Yeah? I'll look into it, then."

Maybe I'll even break down and finally get a smartphone, so we can text translate.

I get my guitar out and sit cross-legged on his bed. Oleg stays where he is, watching me with the same intensity he watches me perform. I watch him watch me, and try out the song I've been working on. The one about sex. With him. I have a chorus, but not the verses yet. Not the hook.

I don't sing the words, but they play in my head as I try out the notes.

I'm up against the wall / your hands tangled in my clothes

I'm kissing, I'm biting, I'm begging for more

Knowing once this rocket's launched, it will never be restored

Knowing once this rocket's launched, you'll never bring me more.

Inspiration isn't mine at the moment, though. I'm too clogged up with the intensity of last night and this morning. The fuzzy-headedness of my on-going denial about it all. I'm very good at compartmentalizing.

Instead, I pick out the tune to Van Morrison's "Brown-Eyed Girl." I don't know why that particular song came out—it's a song my dad used to play for me when I was little. He said it was my song because my eyes are brown. I think it always made me feel loved.

And that's how I feel right now, playing under Oleg's smoldering gaze. If only I could string together all the little moments of feeling loved in my life. Weave them into a tapestry that stays.

But it doesn't. I know better than to believe it would.

I close my eyes and sing the words softly, sinking into the melody. My fingers slide over the frets by memory, knowing the notes by feel. By heart.

Oleg can't sing along, and yet I swear, I feel him listening. Drinking in every note. Every word. Weaving the same sense of pleasure I feel into the music. My pleasure, his. His, mine.

When I stop playing, I open my eyes and look at him.

MY PHONE RINGS from my bag by the door. Oleg gets up and fastens his pants. He retrieves my phone and looks at the screen. Flynn's photo flashes on the front. For a moment, I think he might not let me answer it, but he hands it to me.

"Hey," I answer, looking up at Oleg. My stomach contracts as reality barrels back in.

"Hey." Flynn's voice sounds froggy with sleep. "I was just making sure you're all right. I tried calling last night when I saw your car was still there."

"You did? I'm sorry, I didn't hear it," I lie. I'm actually touched that party-boy brother is checking up on me. It's almost always the other way around. I'm freaking out about him the next day because I left a party at 4 a.m., and he was still there, tripping his balls off.

"Well, you're fine, I just wanted to check. I don't need the details."

"Yeah, everything's cool." I don't know why I check Oleg's face again. Is it cool? Are things going to be cool for him? I actually don't know the real answer. I do know when I tried to leave, he stopped me. But then I quickly forgot because he made me come twice.

"Okay. See ya later."

"Yep. Bye." I hang up.

Oleg nods like he approves. Whether he approves that Flynn's checking up on me or whether he approves of my answer, I can't be sure.

I get up and walk to the bathroom. "I'm going to take another shower," I tell Oleg.

I'm only slightly disappointed that he doesn't follow me in. I really don't think I could take more sex at this point. The guy is huge and rough, and I'm definitely sore.

Even so, I'm already excited to do it all over again. I can't wait to experiment in this new way. To play his bad girl. Receive his punishment and dominance with the pleasure of being wrapped up in his arms when it's over. Something I never wanted before.

I'm definitely like a cat when it comes to men. I want

them on my own terms. I go to them when I want. Leave when I want. I'm the opposite of clingy. So the fact that I would even like being held after sex is freaking weird. But the sex was intense.

So is Oleg.

Maybe that's the addiction.

I turn on the water and take a long shower, refusing to work through the unwelcome thoughts bumping around in my head. I was too shocked last night to examine everything, and now I don't want to.

Oleg's in trouble. I know that much. Someone wants something from him. First they attacked him in front of my place. Then they found him at Rue's. And they grabbed me to try to force him into a car. Which means I'm his weak spot. I'm the leverage on him.

It's stupid that I'm flattered by that. But what's more stupid is how much I want to stay here with him. How much I believe this is my problem, too. That we're in this together.

But there's no together if he can't—or refuses to—explain things to me.

And there shouldn't be together anyway because I don't plan on sticking around long enough to make this a relationship.

Oleg

Story puts her clothes from last night back on and pulls one of my button-downs out of the closet to wear over her tiny t-shirt. "Is it okay if I wear this?"

I nod, absurdly pleased to see my clothes on her body. She leaves it hanging open, like a long jacket.

"So if that's your closet, what's this?" She pulls open the door to the rest of the penthouse.

From the living room, the sounds of voices and baby Benjamin fussing like he's about to fall asleep reach us.

Story's mouth falls open in an exaggerated "O".

"Who's down there?" she says in an exaggerated stage whisper. She stage-tiptoes like she's in a Scooby Doo episode.

I hesitate. Selfish me wants to keep Story to myself. Plus, I haven't told the guys about what happened last night. And I should have. Ravil will have my balls for the omission, but he may have my balls when he finds out my past, anyway, so it's a lose-lose.

She runs down the hall on the balls of her bare feet like a little kid, stopping at the end to peek around the corner into the living room.

I crowd behind her, my arm wrapping around her waist. My head is thick, still aching at times from the concussion.

"You don't live alone," she says with a wondering voice. "That explains the lack of kitchen in your room."

I nudge her out into the open.

The living room is it's usual gathering place. Dima sits at his computer in front of the television. Pavel's on the couch watching with him. Maxim and Sasha are in the kitchen. Nikolai eats at the breakfast counter. Ravil has Benjamin on his shoulder, and he's dancing in front of the wall of windows that look out over Lake Michigan.

Sasha sees us first and gives a cry of delight. She turns off the blender she's running to make a smoothie. "Story's in the house!"

She and Maxim are in their running clothes, probably just back from a jog. Sasha, who is as friendly and social as I am silent, met Story at Rue's the night they all decided to come along to see the girl I'd fallen for. She made sure Story knew my name and wasn't a total creeper.

Pavel turns off the television and swivels to look at us. "Oleg, you animal."

"Shut up," Sasha says, which is good because I was saying the same thing with my glare. "Here, let me do introductions again because you probably don't remember. I'm Sasha, this is my husband Maxim. Nikolai and Dima are twins, if you hadn't guessed. Pavel's on the couch, sexting his girlfriend in L.A. who he saw just a few hours ago, and that's Ravil with the baby. This is his place."

A very diplomatic way of saying that Ravil is our boss. Sasha has such an easy way of speaking, and so does Maxim. Now that they've come to love each other, they've become quite a power couple. Especially with her money and his strategy.

Ravil looks over, Benjamin still sounding off on his shoulder. Even with the distraction, his gaze is shrewd. I've never brought anyone to the penthouse in the entire time I lived here. I don't socialize. I don't go out, other than to Rue's.

"So this is Story," he says lightly. He doesn't walk over, just keeps bouncing the baby. "Sorry I haven't been out to hear you play yet. I'm Oleg's boss."

Story waves. "Nice to meet you all—again. This place is incredible!" She gestures toward the lake view.

I pull out a stool at the breakfast bar for her to sit on. She must be getting hungry for lunch after all that sex. I know I am.

"I thought I heard a guitar playing this morning, but I figured it was someone's radio. How was the show last night?" Sasha quizzes Story.

Story shoots me a glance. I give the tiniest shake of my

head, which she seems to understand. "It was good. Yeah." She doesn't say a word about the men I killed.

I go into the kitchen and pull out the makings for a sandwich, then hold them up with a questioning face.

"Sandwich? I'd love one, thanks."

Sasha and Maxim exchange a look, like they think it's amazing I'm making a sandwich. Or maybe that I'm offering to make someone else a sandwich. Or just that I'm communicating.

"Would you like a mango smoothie?" Sasha offers, holding up the blender.

"Sure. Thanks."

Sasha pours Story a glassful and leans her elbows on the breakfast bar across from Story.

Ravil gets Benjamin to sleep and walks over to shake Story's hand. "Who's this sweet baby?" she coos in a soft voice, so as to not wake him.

Ravil rotates, so Story can see the baby's tiny slumbering face. "This is Benjamin. He's four months old today."

"Happy four-month birthday, little guy," Story sing-songs in a breathy baby voice, lightly rubbing his back. "Congratulations, he's angelic."

I'm transfixed by her. How beautiful she looks talking to the baby. How easy and natural everything is for her. I've lived with these people for two years—the men are my *bratva brothers*—and she seems more comfortable than I feel with them after one minute.

I fix two sandwiches and slice up an apple then bring them on two plates to Story.

"Thank you. My wife is getting a massage in the bedroom right now, but hopefully you'll meet her soon."

"With Natasha?" Nikolai interjects. "I think I'll schedule with her as well."

Dima's head jerks around, and he glares at his brother. "What are you talking about?"

"A massage." Nikolai sounds a bit too innocent. There's some fuckery going on between the twins that the rest of us aren't privy to. "That sounds nice. I think I'll schedule with Natasha, too."

"What, *for you*?" Dima practically explodes.

"Yeah. Unless you're going to." He raises his brows in question.

"I will fucking kill you." I've never heard Dima make a threat. Especially not to his brother.

"Whoa. Okay." Ravil clears his throat. "Sounds like you two have some shit to work out."

"No, I think we're good." Nikolai picks up a magazine from the coffee table and pretends to read it. "Unless he wants me to make that appointment for him instead."

Dima switches to Russian. "I will seriously throw you off the rooftop if you fucking say a word to her."

Ravil shrugs. "Glad we didn't have twins. I'll be back after I put him down."

"So, do you *all* live here?" Story asks, pulling the plate in front of her and scooting her stool over to make room for mine. Maxim and Sasha pull up bar stools opposite ours.

"Yep. It was just the guys and then Lucy—Ravil's wife—moved in. And then Maxim brought me here from Moscow," Sasha explains. "It was an arranged marriage, but I've decided to keep him." She winks.

"I guess you can never get bored with so much going on."

"No." Sasha laughs. "I like it. I was an only child growing up, so it's nice to have people around all the time."

Story smiles. "I grew up in total chaos. Two siblings, a mother who is… emotionally unstable, and a dad who partied like a rock star. We had a lot of love but not much consistency. Consequently, I have a very high tolerance for chaos."

"So, *was* your dad a rock star?" Maxim asks. "Do you take after him?"

Story's laugh is chagrined. "He thinks so. He has a classic rock cover band that's been playing Chicago since the early eighties. The Nighthawks?"

It bothers me that I didn't know this about her. That I haven't been able to make this easy, comfortable conversation. *Blyad'*, until this week, I really didn't give a shit about not being able to communicate. In fact, I sort of preferred it. I still do, so this is making my head ache with conflicting desires.

Maxim shakes his head. "I don't know them. So that's where you and your brother learned to play?"

"Yep. My dad taught guitar lessons in the living room when I was a kid."

"What were you playing this morning? That was an oldie, right?" Sasha asks.

"Van Morrison—yes. My dad used to play it for me because I have brown eyes."

Sasha studies Story. "What color is your hair naturally?"

Story tsks. "*Pink*," she says like she's offended Sasha doesn't think it's natural. "Just kidding, it's dirty blonde."

"I love your look," Sasha tells her. "You really rock the rockstar."

Story's lips quirk. "*Rock the Rockstar.* I might steal that for a song."

"Feel free." Sasha beams like they're best friends.

It's wrong how badly I want them to be. How much I want Story to stay.

"And play away while you're here. We love your music," Maxim says.

Finished with my sandwich, I stand and move closer to Story, putting my hand on her back. Drinking in these delicious morsels about her life. Story leans into me, tipping her head to rest it against my chest. Maxim and Sasha exchange another look, like they can't believe I'm cuddling someone. Or maybe that someone is cuddling with me.

It does seem strange and fantastic that Story just accepted me. We went from strangers to lovers in the blink of an eye.

Relationships always end quickly for me.

She believes this will end as quickly as it started. Maybe that's her M.O. with men—quick to let them in, quick to throw them out. That seems to fit with her enigmatic personality.

As much as the thought of this ending shreds me, something staunch and stubborn rises up. I will still be hers. I won't stop coming to her shows. I will always be whatever she needs me to be for her. Even if it's just the guy in the audience she can trust to climb onto during her shows.

I drop a kiss on her head, and she smiles up at me. I kiss her again, this time on her forehead.

"I'm glad you two finally got together," Sasha says with a warm smile.

Story's gaze drops. "Yeah."

I bring my hand to her nape and gently squeeze. *It's okay,* I want to tell her. No pressure. *You're mine whether you claim me back or not.*

CHAPTER 8

*S*tory

I end up hanging out for another hour with Oleg and his friends in the living area, meeting Ravil's wife, Lucy, when she comes in from a swim. Apparently this millionaire pad has a heated pool and hot tub on the roof. I'm tempted to ask Oleg if we can go skinny-dipping, but I'm starting to get antsy.

But the longer the day goes on, the more I feel like I need to get back to my place. I have classes to teach tomorrow. Or maybe that's just my excuse. I also have this underlying, nagging anxiety to leave. It's the nudge I get when relationships get to a certain stage. This one got here faster than most, but it's been more intense than most. We packed a couple months into the past week.

"Well, I should be going." I swivel to slide off the barstool I've been perched on since lunch.

Oleg blocks my way, concern written on his face.

I change direction and slide off on the opposite side, nimbly taking a quick-step in the direction of Oleg's room. "It was so great hanging out with you guys." I turn and wave at the group. Oleg is right behind me.

I head back down the hallway to his room and slide my feet into my boots again. I pick up my coat and guitar.

Oleg shakes his head.

"Oleg, I can't stay here forever."

He doesn't move, but he's blocking the door.

"Can you drive me to my place?"

He hesitates then shakes his head.

"That's cool," I say, pulling out my phone. "I'll schedule a Lyft."

Oleg takes my phone away from me.

"Hey." I get that he can't talk, but he's pushing it.

He cups my face with so much tenderness, I can hardly stay mad.

"I really need to go."

A half-baked idea forms. Knowing he doesn't seem to want his friends to know what happened last night, I whirl and dart through the door back to the living room then throw open the door to the elevator hallway from there.

Oleg's right behind me, but as I'd guessed, he doesn't catch or stop me.

The elevator door is open, and I step into it. I press the button as Oleg hefts his body between the doors to block them from closing.

He shakes his head at me.

"I can't stay here forever, Oleg. I'm feeling cooped up, and you haven't told me what's going on." I give him a pointed look.

To his credit, he draws back slightly. Like communicating hadn't even occurred to him.

"I don't want to have this fight with you," I tell him, even though we're really not having a fight. We're so much sweeter to each other than most people I know, even when we're at odds.

He shakes his head again, eyes rounding at the word *fight*.

But he refuses to move. He holds the door open and tips his head in the direction of his room.

"Uh uh. I really have to leave now. I have lessons to give tomorrow."

He raps his knuckles against the door and tips his head again. I get the feeling he's trying to appear non-threatening, which is hard for a guy of his size and stature to do. I saw how imposing he was to my errant student at my apartment, and all he had to do there was fold his arms across his massive chest.

My throat works. "You don't want me to leave."

The elevator dings its annoyance.

He beckons to me again. This stand-off is getting really old.

He steps in and takes my guitar, then very gently tips me up over his shoulder. He stops the elevator doors from shutting with my foot. His hand molds over my ass. Not a spank this time, this just feels possessive. I kick my legs. "Dammit, Oleg. This isn't cool."

He carries me down the hall toward the door that enters directly to his bedroom.

"You need to talk to me," I warn, my voice clogged. "I don't know how, but you have to tell me what the fuck is going on. I'm not up for the guessing game anymore."

Oleg stops. He stands there in the hallway, unmoving. Holding me captive over his shoulder.

Oleg

Blyad'.

My life is ugly. I've never been proud of any of it, but I've done what I had to do to stay alive. Still, exposing it to my little swallow is something else. She will run so fast the pavement will light on fire beneath her feet.

And if I'm going to let this darkness out, if I'm going to tell Story about my past, I should come clean with my cell brothers, as well. Own up to my betrayal by omission. I knew this day would come at some point, and every day that went on, I wished it wouldn't. Because I've come to care about this family. I trust them. I rely on them.

And now they will find out they can't trust me.

But for Story, I'm willing to risk losing everything I have here. She said we were having a fight, which terrified me. I can't stand the idea of her mad at me. This girl is the heart that beats in my fucking chest. Hurting her or even pissing her off is the last thing I want to do.

I change direction and walk back to the door to the penthouse, carrying Story inside.

"Um… pretty sure if she wants to go you have to let her," Nikolai says from the breakfast bar where he's working on his laptop. I lower Story to her feet and go for the notepad of paper and pen on the breakfast bar, pushing it beside Nikolai.

I start to write a note to her—but it's rudimentary and crude. I don't speak, and I'm also no writer. Nikolai reads and translates the note over my shoulder. "I can't let you leave. I'm so sorry, Story."

"Um, what the fuck, Oleg?" Nikolai says. His twin stands up from his work table to walk over, texting as he does. Probably telling everyone else to come to the living room.

Story holds up her hand, eyes on my paper, even though she can't read it.

I scribble on the paper. Nikolai reads it. "You're in danger because of me. You must stay here where I can protect you."

Story nods. "Okay, that's what I thought. The people after you know you care about me. That's why they waited at Rue's."

I meet her eye and nod. I'm grateful and shocked by how much Story understood without being told. And she still didn't run away screaming last night.

Sure enough, Sasha and Maxim emerge from their room, and Ravil comes out, too.

"Which people are after you?" Nikolai asks.

"Am I to understand that the men Maxim dispatched last week weren't after Sasha?" Ravil's tone is dangerous.

I nod.

"When were you going to tell me?" Ravil wants to know.

I go blank-faced—my usual default when I don't want to engage. Being mute normally makes it easy to dodge questions.

"Who waited at Rue's?" Ravil turns his quiet authority on Story.

"Some guys. Russian. They seemed like they were waiting for me," Story says. "Out the back door, in the parking lot. Oleg…" —her throat works as she swallows— "um, Oleg took care of them."

Maxim sends me a grim look. To Story, he says gently, "I'm sorry you had to see that."

Ravil pins me with an assessing gaze. After a moment of charged silence, he says, "Story, I need to have a word alone with Oleg."

"No." Story steps closer to me. I tuck her into my side. "I'm a part of this now, and I need to know what it is," Story asserts.

Maxim shakes his head. "No, doll. Everything you hear

puts you more in danger. We'll help you two communicate, but—"

"I'm a part of it." My *shalun'ya* lifts her chin in challenge.

"Oleg?" Ravil asks me.

Fuck. Of course, I don't want her to hear any of it. But as she pointed out, she's already a part of it. And I'm incapable of denying her much of anything. She said we were in a fight because I hadn't told her what was going on.

I nod.

"All right." He waves an arm toward the office. "Max." Ravil orders Maxim to follow, and the four of us troop into Ravil's office, where he closes the door and takes a seat behind his desk. Maxim sinks into the chair in the corner. I yank a chair over beside mine for Story, but she drops into my lap instead. My arms band around her, pulling her in close as I adjust my wounded leg away from her weight. It's a hot, throbbing point of pain at the moment, making it hard to stay focused.

Ravil considers me for a moment. "In the two years since you've been with me, you've never talked about your past."

I don't move.

"I know you spent twelve years in a Siberian prison on a drug charge. I believed you were with the bratva before that, and they had cut out your tongue, but now I'm not so sure. I do know that while on the inside, you acted as enforcer for bratva members. Timofey Gurin wrote your introduction to me."

I make no movement. There wasn't a question, and I can't speak to fill silences. Story toys with my fingers where they lie on her thigh, squeezing my thumb.

"I assumed you were running from something or you wouldn't have left Russia. I'd thought it was your old cell. The introduction would've worked just as easily in Moscow.

Or St. Petersburg. Or Kazan. But you came here to a country where you didn't know the language. To work for me, a *pakhan* you'd never met."

Another pause for silence to settle.

"You refused to say who cut out your tongue."

It's true. He asked me point-blank at least three times when I first arrived, and I stonewalled him, like I stonewall everyone.

"Either it was cut out as punishment for something you already told, or it was to keep you from talking in the future."

When I remain passive, he snaps, "*Tell me which.*"

I scramble to pull out my phone and text him.

He reads the text aloud. "*Future.* That was my guess. So now someone's come around to get your secrets out of you, is that it?"

I nod.

"And they figured out that Story is leverage."

I drop my forehead against her shoulder, the pain of my situation flowing fresh again.

There's a long pause, then Ravil asks, "Who cut out your tongue, Oleg?"

I don't move to answer him. I need his help. His protection. If he throws me out, Story and I will be sitting ducks. I may excel at killing, but even the simplest things are difficult for me without being able to communicate. But my answer will also damn me. He may get rid of me anyway.

There's a huge bounty on Skal'pel'. Clearly on me now, too. People must think I know how to get to Skal'pel'. Or know the new identities of his past clients. Maybe someone is looking for a particular client—who knows why I'm suddenly on the radar.

Story watches me even more closely than Ravil.

"It was an interesting choice, cutting your tongue out. Did they frame you for the drug charge, too?"

I jerk with surprise at the question, giving Ravil the answer he sought.

"You see, to me, it shows a certain affection. Why not simply kill you? Unless this was a person adverse to murder. But considering your training and skill with all manner of weapons, not just your fists, I doubt that was the case. You didn't learn what you know in prison."

My heart thuds painfully in my chest. I tighten my hold on Story, who attempts to soothe me by lightly trailing her fingernails across my inked forearm.

"Am I right? There was love between you. He opted to silence you rather than kill you. And so you keep his secrets."

I let out a shaky breath. Is that true?

Blyad'. I don't know. Maybe it is. I came from nothing. I was nothing. Skal'pel' gave me a home and a job when I was still an eager-to-please youth. He made me feel like a man when I was just teetering on the edge of adulthood. He was a father figure when I had none. In return, I was loyal as hell.

I'd thought that loyalty died when he ruined me, but maybe some of it is still there.

No.

I shake my head.

"No, you're not keeping his secrets?"

I stare at Ravil suddenly feeling sick. I guess I am keeping them. But it wasn't a conscious choice. I can't fucking speak! Except I think Ravil might be right. Some part of me might still be protecting Skal'pel' and, by default, his clients. Loyalty is a character trait I don't know how to turn off.

Ravil laces his fingers and rests them against his chin. "If

114

I made you choose, Oleg, between me and him, who would it be?"

Story twists to look me in the face. I don't expect the mountain of grief that pours over me, even though I'm sure of my answer. It's grief over what Skal'pel' did to me. The pain of betrayal from a man who was like a father to me.

I point at Ravil.

No contest. He's the better man, a hundred times over.

"Good." There's sympathy in Ravil's gaze. Like he sees my pain. "Then you have my protection. Story, too, that goes without saying."

"But?" Story demands.

Ravil raises his brows.

"It sounded like there was going to be a *but*."

She's right, it did.

Ravil shrugs. "But if and when I need you to spill, you'll spill."

I'm sweating but cold. I stare at Ravil.

"I don't give a fuck who you worked for, Oleg," he tells me, and I can suddenly breathe again. "You've never crossed me. Your fierce loyalty is part of who you are. I'm not going to fault you or read more into you still being loyal to someone who fucked you."

The room seems to spin. I don't know why I want to cry like a fucking baby.

Story seems to sense it because she nuzzles her face into my neck and nibbles my skin.

Maxim folds his arms across his chest and looks from me to Ravil. "Something tells me you know exactly who he worked for."

Ravil spreads his hands. "I have a guess."

"Please," Maxim prompts. "I can't fix if I don't know what the fuck we're dealing with."

Ravil looks his way. "Have you gotten a good look at Oleg's tongue?"

Story tightens her hand on my thumb, turns her face into my neck in solidarity.

Maxim shoots me a look and rubs his nose, knowing it's a touchy subject for me.

Ravil answers his question, which apparently was rhetorical. "I have. And it looked pretty damn clean. Not a rough cut. No visible scar tissue. Almost like it got cauterized. Or was done by laser."

Laser. That never occurred to me, but it makes sense. I didn't wake up with a mouthful of blood. A cut would've caused me to choke on my own blood. I woke up with a stub. It was swollen and terribly sore, but it didn't bleed.

Story swallows, pulling back to eyeball me. I pull her in closer.

I'm all right, I want to tell her.

She seems to understand because she nods.

"So how many doctors do we know who worked on the wrong side of the law? Black market surgeries? Maybe identity changes?"

"*Blyad'*," Maxim curses. "*Skal'pel'.* You worked for Skal'pel'?"

I don't answer.

Maxim gets up and walks over. He puts his hand on my shoulder. "You can tell me. I don't give a fuck what you did in the past, either. You're my brother now."

I blink at the smarting in my eyes and nod.

"So I'm guessing you can identify at least twenty guys the bratva wants dead." Maxim says.

I shrug. Maybe. It wasn't my job to memorize faces or names—not the old ones, nor the new ones. But yeah, maybe.

"And you don't know where your old boss disappeared to?" Ravil asks.

I shake my head.

"I'm going to find him for you, Oleg," Maxim promises. "And if you won't kill him for what he did to you, I will."

I acknowledge the unease that brings me. I don't want to kill him. At least, I didn't before.

Have I been waiting all these years for him to contact me? To take me back?

It seems insane, but I think some part of me was. Like I still belonged to that cruel father figure. I hadn't forgiven him, but I was waiting.

Story presses the back of her hand to my neck, then her lips to my head. She turns to look at Ravil. "I know this conversation is important, but he needs a doctor. Oleg's burning up."

CHAPTER 9

*S*tory

Ravil stands. "Get Svetlana," he says to Maxim, who pulls out his phone to text. To me, he explains, "She's a midwife who lives in the building. She should carry antibiotics."

I want to hold Oleg. Not because of the fever although I'm worried about that. But because whatever just went down in this office seemed big. Important to him. And I still don't understand any of it.

I'm part relieved, part frustrated to see that Oleg's walls aren't just for me. They're for everyone around him—including the people he lives with and apparently loves.

Ravil called him fiercely loyal, and I realize that's what he's been to me, as well. He decided at some point to become my number one fan, and then nothing would sway him from that job. Now he has to be my protector.

His loyalty to me makes me feel it right back. I may normally be flighty and flakey in relationships—at least the intimate ones—but there was no question when I found him bleeding in my van that I was all-in with him. And no ques-

119

tion when we got jumped at Rue's. Whatever he's into, I'm sticking beside him.

Once we see it through, I'll probably bail, but I don't abandon friends in need.

He's more than a friend, a voice whispers in my head.

I nuzzle into his neck and kiss his hot skin. "You should go and lie down," I murmur.

No. He doesn't move, but I hear the word clearly projected in my head.

I stand and pull on his hand. "Come on. Svetlana will need to look at your wound."

He catches me around the waist and lifts me back to his lap. With his phone, he texts one-handed and sends a message.

Ravil's phone beeps. He reads the message and considers me.

"What does it say?" I demand. This literal game of telephone is going to drive me nuts.

"It says, *talk to Story*." Ravil says it like an apology. Like he already knows it's going to piss me off, and it does.

I rotate to glare at Oleg. "I told you not to do that."

His stare back is blank. I want to slap that impassive wall right down. "Oleg. what the fuck, does *talk to Story* mean?" I demand.

"I'm guessing he wants us to straighten out the issue of you wanting to leave the premises," Maxim says mildly from beside us.

Oleg nods.

Okay, that makes sense. But I'm still pissed. "Don't say *talk to Story*," I tell Oleg. His stoicism crumbles under my glare. He blinks. His lips move. I swear to God he mouths the word *sorry*.

"Was that *sorry*?" I ask.

He nods. He looks sorry.

"Thank you." My shoulders sag. I point at my sternum. "*You* talk to me. Don't make them do it for you. I don't even know them."

I barely know Oleg, I think, but then acknowledge it's not true. I know him intimately. And I feel like I've always known him.

Oleg appears daunted. I don't think he's breathing. He looks at his phone and back at me. Then he types something.

Ravil reads it. "I need you to stay here. Please, *lastochka*." Ravil looks at Maxim. "What bird is that in English?

Maxim clears his throat. "Swallow."

Swallow. He has a pet name for me. And I'd never heard it. But like any songbird, I hate to be caged. The anxiety I feel before I break things off with a guy rears up strongly. "I have lessons to teach, starting tomorrow. And gigs Friday and Saturday."

Yeah, I'm being irrational. I had a gun to my head last night. I shouldn't be thinking about lessons and gigs.

Oleg scowls and shakes his head.

Maxim interjects, "Sorry, sweetheart. You're going to sit tight while we figure out who's after you and Oleg and make it go away."

"That's right," Ravil says. "I hate to paint the picture for you, but I will. Someone wants what's in Oleg's head, and they know he cares about you, which means your life's in danger. Unless you want to get picked up and tortured while Oleg watches, you'll stay where we can protect you. I'm not going to elaborate on what would happen after they got what they wanted, if Oleg can even give it to them."

A muscle tics in Oleg's cheek. He sucks in a harsh breath through his nostrils.

"Right. Okay." My voice sounds shaky. That makes sense. I twist my fingers around each other. "Um, yeah. I'll cancel my lessons."

"You will." Ravil walks around to the front of his desk and leans against it.

"But what about the gigs this weekend? I don't have a replacement."

Oleg growls his displeasure.

"You'll cancel them, too, if we don't have this sorted out," Ravil says.

Maxim gets up to pace. "Who came after you on Saturday?" he asks Oleg. "Did you know them?"

Oleg shakes his head and types on his phone. Ravil reads the text aloud in English. *I didn't recognize anyone. They seemed like bounty-hunters.* "Who wants you?" Ravil asks.

Oleg shrugs and types again. *Could be anyone who found out who I worked for. They want to know where to find him, probably. Or where to find one of his associates.*

"And do you know?" Ravil asks.

Oleg shakes his head and types, *it's been twelve years. I was in prison and with you. I know nothing.*

"But whoever is after you will probably keep trying," Maxim asks.

Oleg nods.

"Well, maybe the best defense is a good offense," Maxim says.

No. I hear Oleg say it with his whole being before I even understand what they're talking about. He didn't speak or shake his head, but his body goes rigid, and his hands tighten on me.

Apparently Maxim is also practiced at reading Oleg's non-communication. "You know I'm right."

Oleg shakes his head.

"Wait...what are we talking about?" I ask.

Ravil catches his hands loosely in his lap. "We're talking about using you as bait, Story."

Cold washes over me, especially when Oleg holds me like someone's trying to rip me from his arms.

"If we don't get who's behind these attacks, we can't stop them from happening. You'll be hiding here forever, and you've already said you're not up for that." Ravil looks at Oleg. "We'll all go to the gig. And I won't let anyone touch her. We just need to take someone alive, so we can question them. Find out who wants you and what information they're after. Get to the bottom of this." He glances at Maxim who holds up his hands in surrender.

"I know. My fault for dispatching the first three without getting answers first. I fucked up," Maxim admits.

Oleg shakes his head.

Oh God, I'm so out of my mind. "Yes," I answer. "Let's do it." I can't cancel the gigs. There's no one who can replace me, and I don't want to leave the bars in the lurch. It's unprofessional. Anxiety churns in my stomach, but I trust these guys to protect me. Oleg alone is a formidable bodyguard. He rescued me when he was outgunned, and I was already in the enemy's hands. If all of his gang or friends or whatever are going to be there, I'll probably be safe.

Besides, I can't stay here longer than this week. I can practically sense the time-bomb for our relationship ticking down. Every minute I stay, I sink in deeper with Oleg, which will only make things harder when they end.

I slide to my feet. "So I stay until Friday, and then you'll take care of the problem," I sum up. "And I can go back to my normal life."

Oleg rises, his brows down over his eyes.

A knock sounds at the door. Dima opens the door to let a

slender young woman in her twenties with strawberry blonde hair in. He follows her.

"Natasha," Ravil says. He sounds slightly surprised.

The name sounds familiar, but it takes a moment for me to figure out why. Then I remember—Natasha was the massage therapist Dima and Nikolai were arguing over.

"Sorry, I know you were expecting my mom. She's out delivering a baby, but she got Maxim's message and asked me to bring this up." The young woman holds up a large bottle of pills. "She said to tell you she will come and check on whomever has the infection." The young woman darts a glance at me. "Hey."

"Hi." I walk forward and take the pills. "Is the dosage on here?"

"She said to take one now, and one before bed if she's not here by then." Natasha cocks her head. "Are they for you?"

I tip my head in Oleg's direction. "They're for Oleg. He has a wound. I'm guessing it's infected. I hope that's all it is."

"May I see it? I could make a poultice. I've been assisting my mom since I was in grade school, and I'm a licensed massage therapist. I'm into all the natural remedies. I have teas, tinctures, essential oils, salves—you name it."

I glance at Oleg for his agreement. Of course, as usual, nothing shows on his face, so I make the decision for him. "Yeah, that would be great."

Oleg takes a step but loses his balance, throwing a hand out to catch the chair, which he nearly knocks over.

Natasha stumbles back into Dima, who catches her with an arm around her waist and a hand at her hip.

"Little help," I call out, ducking under Oleg's arm to support his massive body, but he recovers his balance on his own. I notice Dima hasn't released Natasha yet. He lowers his head as if to kiss the top of hers or smell her hair but stops an inch away. His lids droop like having his hands on her is an unexpected pleasure. He doesn't release her until she turns into him, blushing, and mumbles something I don't understand. It sounded like, "*Spasibo*."

Interesting. Someone has a crush.

"Are you Russian, too?" I ask as I follow her out the door. Dima holds it open then leads the way down the hall, as if we needed an escort.

"Yes," she smiles.

"Is everyone in this building Russian?" I say it as a joke, but Natasha nods, smiling.

"Yes. That's why it's known as the Kremlin. Ravil only rents to Russians and at rates we wouldn't find anywhere in the city." She throws a grateful glance over her shoulder at Ravil, who has left the office behind us. "He takes care of his own."

He takes care of his own. Yes, like any mafia leader. He's mild-mannered, but I could tell by the tension in Oleg when he questioned him, that he respects and holds his boss in high regard. Ravil wields his power quietly.

They're killers, all of them. Dangerous men in dangerous business. I keep trying to shove that into a box and forget it, but there's an anxiety gnawing in the background. I have a high threshold for trauma and chaos, but this is all starting to get to me. My compartmentalizing skills are starting to fray.

As we walk, I notice Oleg favors his leg a bit. He's not limping, but there's a stiffening through his trunk when he walks on it. Christ, why didn't I notice sooner that he hasn't healed? There's been so much to decipher and interpret and try to understand since he brought me here. I feel way out of my depth with all of it.

I squeeze his hand, and he looks down at me. It's faint—

barely perceptible—but I see the shadow of a smile at the corners of his lips.

I don't want to think about where this is going. How close I'm starting to feel with him because I need to brace against this becoming anything real. I can't start to believe this is going to last. It can't. He's Russian mafiya. I'm allergic to relationships. This can't work.

Still, that ghost of a smile produces that same swirling warmth I always felt as Saturdays approached, and I knew he'd be there to watch me. Up for anything I threw his way—standing on his table. Climbing on his shoulders. Making him catch me as I dead-dropped off the stage.

We pass through the living room and kitchen toward Oleg's room. Dima is still with us, leading the way. "So, what's your connection here?" Natasha asks, which I realize is a nice way of asking who I am. I never introduced myself.

"I'm Story. A friend of Oleg's."

"Nice to meet you."

"You, too."

Dima opens the door and steps inside. We all follow, but Oleg hesitates, standing in the middle of his room.

"Pants off, big guy," I tell him. He toes off his boots and unbuttons his jeans.

"Oh, um. Where is the wound?" Natasha asks.

Dima steps closer like he's going to shield her from any unwanted peen if it gets flashed.

Oleg sways on his feet again, and I move in to help him carefully get his jeans down over his wound and then sit down.

For fuck's sake. The bandage is soaked with yellow and red, and when Natasha kneels beside him and gently peels it back, we both gasp. The edges of the wound are swollen and angry, and puss is coming out of it. I look away, suddenly nauseated.

"Okay, wow. Definitely infected. Give him one of those antibiotics for starters." Natasha indicates the bottle I'm holding.

I jump into action. "Right. Oh my God." My hands shake as I pry it open.

Dima leaves and returns with a glass of water, which he hands to Oleg, who throws the pill back and swallows.

"I'm going to go downstairs and make a poultice. Do you have hydrogen peroxide you can pour over the wound?" Natasha stands.

I look at Dima who nods. "I'll get it."

"Why didn't you tell me you weren't feeling well?" I demand.

Oleg pulls me around to his other side and sits me on his good knee.

"Oh my God! I was sitting on your wound!"

He shakes his head.

"No? You could die from an infection like this. What if you have MRSA? I should have taken you to the hospital when it happened."

Oleg shakes his head lightly and closes his eyes.

"Oleg?"

His eyes open, and he stares back at me.

"You've probably been feeling miserable this whole time. Why didn't you tell me?"

He shakes his head.

"You *have* to start communicating with me."

"I can help with that." Dima reappears with the hydrogen peroxide and a washcloth. He also carries a tablet, which he hands to Oleg. "I have you all set up, my man." He touches the screen, which reveals a keyboard with the Russian alphabet. "You type in here, it spits out the English for Story. It can even speak it aloud although I didn't find a voice with a Russian accent." Dima grins.

I pour the hydrogen peroxide liberally over Oleg's wound, catching the drips with the washcloth. I suck in a breath when it bubbles and hisses over the open wound.

Oleg types something with his forefinger. He's slow. I imagine his large finger makes it harder.

"Hit that to make it speak aloud." Dima points at the screen.

An Australian-accented male voice says, "Don't worry about me, swallow."

I meet his eye. "What was *swallow* in Russian?" I ask.

Oleg looks down at the screen, like he's not sure how to reverse the language, but Dima answers for him. "*Lastochka.* Is that what he calls you? I can set that word not to translate, if it's your pet name." He picks up the tablet and types something in.

Natasha reappears and doctors the wound with a poultice, and then she and Dima leave us alone.

Oleg falls back on the bed. I curl into his side, resting my head on his shoulder. He looks at me and points at my chest then at his own.

"I belong to you?"

A tiny smile appears. I didn't get it right, but he likes my interpretation. He nods.

"Oleg, I—"

He stops my words with a finger on my lips then repeats the gesture, reversing it.

"You belong to me?" His lips tip up again. He nods.

I can't stop staring at him. He looks so transformed with the small smile. Much younger. So warm.

He belongs to me. One part of me wants to reject that gift.

Because believing it's something I can count on is irrational. I know love doesn't last. People don't stick. We just do the best they can as we all muddle through life.

That's what Oleg and I are doing right now. And it's a precious moment, despite—no, *because* of the drama surrounding it.

I want to believe what he's telling me. That this sturdy, steady man will always be there for me. Always and forever. Something I've never had with anyone in my life.

Maybe it could really be true.

CHAPTER 10

Oleg

I pass out for the rest of the afternoon, falling in and out of feverish dreams. The worst kind—the type that picks up right where real life left off, so I can't be sure if they're really happening or not. I know Natasha came back to check on my wound and change the poultice. Dima stood behind her like her bodyguard. Or maybe that was a dream, too.

In one dream, Story walks out of the Kremlin while I'm asleep, and the bearded asshole from Rue's guns her down in cold blood.

In another, Skal'pel' operates on her, removing her tongue, too, so she can never sing again.

Then he's here in my bedroom with a gun on her. I jerk awake, a hoarse cry coming from my lips. I lunge for my gun in my nightstand.

"Hey." Story's voice cuts across the room. "Are you okay?" She's curled up in a chair by the big windows, her guitar across her thighs.

I release my grip on the gun before she can see it, my

131

pulse racing. *Blyad'.* What if I'd pointed it at her before I got my head on straight? The thought does nothing to calm my pounding heart.

Story puts the guitar down and comes to the bed. She has a way of moving that's more childlike than sultry-woman. She skips steps. Leaps onto the bed with a bounce instead of crawling. It's part of what makes her so fascinating to me. She yanks the covers back and tucks her legs into the bed to sit with me then shoves the iPad Dima brought me under my nose.

I stare at it for a moment, remembering what I'm supposed to be doing with it.

I had a bad dream, I type. The Australian *mudak* speaks the words to her.

"What about?" she asks.

I point at her. *I dreamed he cut your tongue out, too.*

Fuck. I feel so raw and exposed giving voice to my nightmare, but Story's been demanding communication from me.

"Scalpel?" she asks.

I nod.

"What was he to you?" Her brown eyes search my face.

Damn. I haven't told this story before, not that I ever talk about my past. But Story, of course, deserves to know. I frown over the letters, using both index fingers to hunt and peck.

When I was fourteen, my mother took a housekeeping job with a wealthy plastic surgeon named Andrusha Orlov. I sometimes helped my mother after school, and the doctor took a liking to me. He paid me to do odd jobs for him and took a fatherly role with me.

"Did you have a father?" Story asks, folding her slender legs underneath her to sit cross-legged.

I shake my head. *I never knew him. He left when I was young.*

"I'm sorry."

I shrug. *When I was seventeen, Dr. Orlov asked me if I wanted a job as his personal bodyguard. I was already almost this size. He had a security team, and the head of it was former military. He trained me to shoot a gun. To fight with my hands. He taught me seventy-two ways to kill a man.*

I didn't know why Orlov needed protection, but I didn't care. I was getting paid more money than my mom made as his housekeeper and feeling like a man. As time continued, he took me to meetings he held with people in public restaurants or bars. I sat in on meetings where large sums of cash changed hands. Over the next five years, I witnessed more and more of Orlov's identity-changing business.

Then things got too hot. The St. Petersburg bratva came after him when they got word he'd performed surgery on a man they wanted dead. I killed three men who showed up at his residence. It scared me.

I tried to quit. He persuaded me to stay just until he closed out his operation, changed his own identity and disappeared.

I stop typing. The rest of the story isn't worth telling.

Story slips her hand in mine. "And he cut out your tongue to thank you."

I rub my aching head and nod.

"Where's your mom?" Story asks.

Pain stabs through my chest. My sweet, honest, hard-working mother. *She lost her job and her son when Skal'pel' left,* I type.

"Does she know you're alive?"

I rub my head again.

"Oleg?" Story leans her head forward to peek at my face.

133

I was too ashamed to see her again. I went straight from prison to Chicago. I needed a new start.

Story leans her head on my shoulder, curling her body against mine, her knees folding over the top of my thighs. "I hate what happened to you." She sounds choked up.

I stroke her cheek, brushing her hair back over her ear. Dredging up my shitty past sucked, but now that it's out— now that Story knows it and Ravil and Maxim know part of it —something that's been blocked all these years has moved. I used my pain as a wall to keep everyone out. To keep myself out. I was half a man, barely living half a life.

I was missing far more than my tongue.

But now that wall is down. The path isn't clear—far from it. There's fucking rubble everywhere. But I'm willing to pick through it.

"You should contact your mom," Story says, threading her fingers through mine. "I'll bet she's dying not knowing about you."

My chest constricts, and I fight a lump in my throat. I nod my agreement.

"Speaking of moms, I need to call mine. She's kind of a mess." Story slips off the bed and retrieves her retro flip-phone.

I type on the iPad, *What happened?* It's strange to have a real conversation with anyone, but Story makes it seem possible.

Story comes back to the bed and sits cross-legged again. "My mom suffers from depression. She's amazing, but totally unreliable as a parent. I'm more the parent in the relationship. I mean, when things are good, she's there for us—for me and Flynn and Dahlia, our baby sister. But her life is a roller-coaster of falling in love and then falling apart. And last time I talked to her, it seemed like things were going south with her boyfriend, Sam. I'm just going to check in with her." Story dials a number on the phone while I type on the iPad.

"Hey, Mom. Just checking in. Give me a call when you get this." Story closes the phone. "Voicemail."

It was hard for you. I pass the iPad to Story. I'm sick of the Australian asshole speaking for me. I'd rather she just read it.

"It was okay. I felt loved. I just couldn't rely on anyone."

You can rely on me, I want to tell her, but I hold back. She's skittish when it comes to commitment, and I'm in no position to push. Not when I can't even keep her safe.

"My dad's life was also pretty crazy with sex, drugs and rock 'n roll. Now I worry that Flynn's going down that path, you know?" Her eyes shine with tears, which she blinks back. "But music is really the one thing we have. It's what holds our family together, even though it's not the most stable unifying force. I couldn't go to college because things were just too crazy with my mom being in and out of psychiatric care. I needed to stay home and make sure Flynn and Dahlia were okay. So my brother and I ended up in a band. Only Dahlia went to school."

What else would you want to do? I type. *If you could?*

Story tosses her phone back in her purse. "I don't know. I've never even thought about it. Maybe I would do nothing different. I love the band. And I like teaching guitar. I really do. It works, you know?"

I study her, trying to decipher whether there's something hidden in there to decode, but my skills at conversation and women are so lacking, I can only take her words at face value.

I try again. *What would you have studied if you'd gone to college?*

"Probably something completely useless like French literature. Or Art History." She shrugs and gives me an impish smile.

I fucking love this girl.

She touches the iPad. "I like talking to you."

You're mine for the next five days, I write. I don't suggest anything more permanent, even though I don't intend to give her up. Ever.

"I guess so. You'd better get better, so we can hang out. I mean, watching you sleep is fun and all, but…"

She wrenches a smile from me. The unfamiliar expression is happening more and more with her around.

I'm already better, I tell her although it's not entirely true. My head aches, and I could probably fall back to sleep again in a heartbeat. *Tomorrow I will wear you out.*

She sucks in a breath and shoots an excited look at me. "Is that dirty talk?"

I nod, and her smile widens. "Oh my God, I can't wait to hear all the filthy thoughts in that big head of yours."

I arch a brow. *Careful what you wish for.*

Story straddles my lap, grinding her warm core over my semi, turning it into a full-fledged boner. "How much better are you feeling?" she purrs.

Well enough to fuck the daylights out of you, shalun'ya, I type, using the non-translate feature on her other pet name, then toss the iPad aside and flip her to her back.

"I hope *shalun'ya* means something very naughty." She tugs up my shirt.

I growl and claim her mouth, showing her exactly how I treat my little minx when she's a bad girl.

CHAPTER 11

O *leg*

I wake to find Story gone.

I fly out of the bed and pound down the hallway in my boxer briefs and t-shirt. The living room is bright with daylight.

Fuck. Did I lose time again? How much?

Vaguely, it comes back to me that I slept through the afternoon and evening. Story stayed with me, playing her guitar softly and moving about the room. I vaguely remember Sasha inviting her to eat—I don't know if it was lunch or dinner. Maybe both.

That must've been yesterday.

"Hey, big guy. How are you feeling?" Nikolai asks from the couch. He's eating donuts from a box on the coffee table.

I throw my arms in the air in frustration, demanding to know where Story went.

"Relax." Maxim emerges from the kitchen drinking a glass of grapefruit juice. "Story's up on the roof with Sasha."

The roof. I shake my head, already reaching for the door.

"They're safe up there—you think I would allow it if they

137

weren't? There's no clear shot onto that roof from any direction. I promise."

I relax my grip on the door handle slightly, debating if I should go put on pants before I storm up there, since it's not an emergency, when I hear screams and the sound of bullets piercing metal from the rooftop.

Everyone in the penthouse flies into action. I fling open the door, running. The footsteps of my brothers pound behind me, Maxim at my neck. Pavel and Nikolai are further back, both with guns drawn. I take the stairs three at a time and throw open the door to the rooftop with a whack. Sasha and Story crouch together in the hot tub, covering their heads.

"They're shooting at us!" Sasha yells to Maxim in Russian.

Maxim whirls, checking the buildings around us, calming the women at the same time. "It's all right," he tells them. "There's no clear shot. I promise you. The places where there might be, we put up bullet-proof glass."

I want to kill Maxim for letting Story out of his sight, but I struggle to let his words seep in. They really aren't in danger.

Ravil and Dima arrive on the roof, also with pistols in hand. A few more shots are fired, I see Maxim was right. They hit the tall HVAC unit, bounce off the bullet-proof windows below.

"Over there." Ravil points to the building beside us that has one of the windows removed. "Get a team in that building now," he barks.

I can't think of anything but getting to Story. I jog to the hot tub and pick up one of the towels lying over a chair to hold out to cover her. She's in nothing but her panties, and I want to murder every one of my bratva brothers for glimpsing her tits, not that they're looking.

She scrambles out and jumps on me, straddling my waist, arms around my neck, soaking my clothes with the hot water. I wrap the towel around her back, holding her tight.

Maxim pulls Sasha out of the tub and into his arms.

I'm still not breathing. Not able to stop the terror rushing through my veins.

"It's a message," Ravil says grimly. "Someone's trying to scare you."

I'm going to kill all of them. Every last person who threatened Story's life. I turn and stalk off the roof, carrying Story like she's the only thing keeping me alive.

"I'm okay," she murmurs in my ear, even though she still clings to me as tightly as when she flung herself into my arms. "It just scared us. We didn't know we couldn't be hit."

My swallow. I never want to put her down again. I carry her into my bedroom and pace in a circle with her.

"I'm okay," she repeats. She leans her cheek against mine. "Your fever broke. Are you feeling better?"

I pace another circle.

"Put me down, big guy. I need to get dressed. Of course, I have no clothes to wear."

I set her gently on the dresser and fish out a long-sleeved t-shirt for her to wear as she peels off her wet panties. She pulls the shirt over her head. The sleeves drape down over her hands, making her look like a rag doll. She laughs and takes her arms out of the sleeves, then pushes them up through the neck hole, bringing it down below her shoulders. She then ties the long sleeves under her breasts, creating the appearance of a strapless shirt-dress. It's bohemian and beautiful. I gather her back up in my arms and kiss her forehead.

"I'm all right," she says again. "Come on, let's get back out there to talk about this."

I know she's right, but I'd rather keep her locked in my bedroom.

Indefinitely.

I'm also extremely distracted knowing she's wearing no panties beneath my t-shirt. My hand covers her ass as we walk out together, my fingertips tracing the curve of her buttocks.

She tips her head up to me and gives me a secret smile.

Everyone's in the living room when we get there. Sasha has also changed into her clothes, and Lucy's standing with baby Benjamin over her shoulder, patting his little diapered butt. Her expression is tight. I'm sure the high-strung lawyer doesn't like any of the bratva violence coming close to her child. It was the reason she tried to hide her pregnancy from Ravil in the first place. Ravil only won her over after abducting her and holding her as his prisoner.

"We were too late. The team found the office building they were shooting from, but the shooter had already escaped," Maxim reports to me.

Fuck.

I catch Sasha's eye and finger Story's makeshift dress and then point to her with a questioning face.

"Story needs some clothes!" Sasha guesses. She beckons to Story. "I meant to get you some when we got out. Come with me." They disappear into the bedroom together, and when they emerge, Story has a pair of leggings underneath my shirt and a pink cropped hoodie sweatshirt to cover her arms. She looks every bit the rockstar she is.

"Listen, I'm going to need to go and get some things if I'm staying here all week," Story says.

Over my dead body she leaves this place. I shake my head.

Maxim and Ravil exchange a look. "It's not a bad idea,"

Maxim says, appealing to me. "We just bump up the plan by going to her apartment. It would be easier to control things there versus at a nightclub."

Story looks at me.

I shake my head at her.

"Story wouldn't necessarily have to go. The two of you could stay here, where they can't touch you. We send a crew to her apartment to get her things. If we see anyone, we take them," Ravil says.

I nod. I'll agree to any plan that doesn't involve Story. I pick up the paper and pencil still on the counter from before and write, *It's hard to see how that would work without me there.* I hand it to Ravil.

He reads it aloud. "True. Then you come. We leave Story here. You're the bait. It's far more simple. We need to get this thing resolved immediately."

"I would like to go, though," Story says. "You know, to figure out what I need."

I shake my head.

"Oleg, you're being irr—"

I cut off Story's argument with a slam of my fist to the wall beside me. I didn't mean to show my aggression, but she's had a gun pointed to her head and now bullets fired at her. There's no fucking way I'm letting her walk into danger again when she doesn't have to.

"*Hey,*" she snaps, her eyes flashing. Clearly she's not afraid of me, which is a relief. In fact, she gets right up in my face—well, as close as she can get to my face considering how much shorter she is than I am—and points her finger. "*Don't* do that again."

I blink at her. I know I should apologize, but I also can't promise it won't happen again. I *am* fucking irrational when it comes to her safety.

"She has more guts than I do," Pavel mutters.

"Right?" Dima answers.

"As if he'd ever hurt her," Sasha scoffs. "You two? You're a different story."

"Story stays." Ravil's authority cuts across any more arguments. "Oleg comes. Maxim, arrange for back up. We'll leave in one hour."

"Not you," Lucy warns, wide-eyed from the corner.

Ravil hesitates, his gaze flicking to his baby boy and his mother.

"*Pakhan* stays," Maxim says, as if he's the boss rather than Ravil. He knows Ravil wouldn't choose to protect himself, though, and his marriage depends on sheltering their family from bratva violence.

I hate myself for bringing this violence upon them.

If I had any decency, I'd leave. Walk out alone, offer myself up to the thugs who want me and free everyone else—especially Story—from the danger I'm dumping on them.

But leaving Story feels like an impossibility. My life began the night I took her home. I woke up from the dead. Wanted to connect. To share.

And so I'm trapped now, between the need to keep Story and the need to protect her.

STORY

I make a list of things I want from my apartment, and the guys leave.

I've seen some crazy shit in my life. I've watched my parents have the kind of fights that involved flying dishes and broken furniture. I've had to check my mom in and out of mental hospitals. I held my brother while he was on a bad drug trip. In middle school, my best friend slit her wrists, and I sat beside her at the hospital.

I consider myself resilient. It's why I didn't totally freak when I found Oleg shot and bleeding in my van. Or when I watched him kill my three attackers. I've built a high tolerance for trauma.

But right now, I'm about as keyed up as I've ever been. My stomach's up in my throat, and I've never felt so helpless. The idea of anything happening to Oleg terrifies me.

I pace the length of windows that look out over the lake in the penthouse living room, too keyed up to even put my thoughts together.

Sasha watches me with sympathy. "He'll be all right. They all will."

I look over to see if she's trying to convince herself. Her fingers are intertwined tightly and she's also standing aimlessly.

But she says, "These guys are badass."

"Yes." I remember how efficient and skilled Oleg seemed to be at Rue's. He knows what he's doing, and he's not alone.

"Do you like to play music when you're trying not to think about something?"

"Yeah."

"Want to get your guitar?"

"You don't mind?"

"Are you kidding? I need the distraction, too."

"What about the baby?" I ask.

Sasha waves her hand. "Oh, we have him trained to sleep through anything."

I go to Oleg's room and get my guitar. When I bring it back, I tune it and strum my fingers without thinking. "What's your favorite?" I ask Sasha.

"Oh, stupid stuff. Top forty. You play what you like."

I play through the Storyteller's entire album on autopilot, just trying to get through it.

"Is that all original music?" Sasha asks when I finish.

I nod, absently. The noise in my head is so loud.

"Do you guys have a manager?"

I laugh. "Yeah, me."

"No, you need a real manager. Someone who will pimp you hard. Get you booked outside of Chicago. If you broaden your reach, I'll bet you could get a recording deal. Seriously."

I'm saved from deflecting her well-meaning advice by the door opening. Oleg comes through first, and I almost fall down with relief.

I drop the guitar, run right over the top of the sofa—one foot on the cushion, the next on the back—and divebomb him, wrapping my legs around his waist.

He catches me and spins me around and pins my back against a wall, claiming my mouth with an intensity that makes my toes curl. When he pulls away, I don't let him, chasing his lips with mine for more. I use my tongue, hoping it won't bother him that he can't use his back. It doesn't seem to. He palms my ass and drops my hips lower, so he can grind the bulge of his erection between my legs.

"They were there, but they caught sight of the rest of us and sped off," I hear Maxim telling Ravil. "Pavel and I chased their car, and we got a plate number. It will be a rental, but maybe Dima can track them."

"Already on it." Dima has somehow teleported to his workstation where his fingers fly across the keys.

Oleg puts me down and carries my things to his room, then we return to the living room, where I curl up on Oleg's lap on the large red sofa. The television gets turned on to Netflix, and Nikolai picks *Arrested Development*. The relief of doing something normal, of having Oleg back, the way he quiets the noise for me is so great that I almost fall asleep.

"Well, I found something. There's a three million dollar reward for bringing Oleg in alive posted on the dark web in Russia," Dima says. "Looks like it might be from another bratva cell." He reads aloud, *Subject: Bratva Enforcer with Ravil Baranov's cell. Residence: well-guarded bratva stronghold, likely impossible to penetrate. Is known to frequent a bar called Rue's Lounge, with a possible love interest there.* And there's a photo of Story on Oleg's table."

A muscle tics in Oleg's jaw.

Dima lifts his head. "I say we turn him in and collect the reward."

Oleg stiffens, head jerking up.

"That's a joke." Dima sobers. "*Gospodi,* Oleg, do you really think we'd sell you out?"

"Put up a notice," Ravil says. "Oleg belongs to me. Anyone who attempts to touch him dies. If anyone wants the information in his head, it's for sale. They can talk to me."

Oleg doesn't seem to be breathing.

"Is that okay?" I murmur for his ears only.

He swallows then nods.

"Put up a notice," Dima mutters, but his face is on the screen, fingers flying over the keys. "That's not exactly how it works, but I understand."

Ravil looks at Oleg. "I already had a call from Kuznets in Moscow. He wants names. Do you have them?"

Oleg shakes his head.

"No names at all? Not a single one?"

He shakes his head again.

"Only faces?"

Oleg nods.

"And it's been years. That's not going to be useful to

anyone. Can you put that up on the dark web?" Ravil asks Dima.

Dima snorts but keeps typing. "I'll put up a notice," he says sarcastically, but he's also bobbing his head, as if he will do whatever he can.

"Will that keep Oleg safe?" I ask.

Ravil nods. "I'll take care of it. No one will touch him without my say-so, which means no one will touch him." A shiver runs up my spine because I can practically feel the danger radiating from Ravil. At least he's on Oleg's side. I'd hate to be on the wrong side of the guy.

CHAPTER 12

*O*leg

"Hey, thanks, man," Flynn says when I set down the heavy amp on the stage of a brew pub Friday night.

I almost walk away without acknowledging his words—like my old self would—but then turn back and nod. Story is changing me. Bringing me back to the living. Communicating. Giving and receiving from the people around me. It's so simple and yet profound.

I'm rewarded with a grin that matches Story's.

I brought Story to the Storyteller's gig, and my entire gang came as back-up, but Ravil believes Story and I are safe now.

According to Dima, all interest in me has come down off the dark web. There are no more contracts out to bring me in. I answered to both Kuznets, the new Moscow *pakhan,* and another bratva boss in Russia. I told them both all I know. I remembered many people who had changed. I just don't know their new identities. I wasn't given some secret USB drive with all the information that I kept with me all these years. After several hours of questioning, both bosses decided I was pretty useless.

This is our test. We're out in public, totally exposed. I'm a live wire, totally on edge, but Story's obvious exuberance at being able to perform makes me hide it for her sake.

After carrying in all the heavy equipment for the band, I find a table on the side of the room. It's not Rue's, so there isn't a spot closer to the stage I can grab, but I have my back to a wall, and I can see everyone, so this works.

Sasha and Maxim drop into chairs beside me. Pavel and Adrian find their own table, Dima and Nikolai take an opposite wall. We're all carrying pieces, not that we'd use them in here.

Sasha orders a Cosmo. Maxim gets Stoli on the rocks. I lift my eyebrows and point when he orders, indicating I'll have the same. I have the iPad Dima gave me with me, though. I could order anything I want.

There's a lightness to that freedom. I don't think I realized how I'd fettered myself by never trying. It's not like Dima couldn't have given me a device ages ago. The guy can pretty much do anything. I just didn't try. Didn't care that I couldn't communicate.

Or I thought I didn't care.

Story's made it important now.

When I'm not checking out the crowd for danger, my eyes track her everywhere she moves. That's a given. If she's in a room, my gaze is glued to her. But it feels different this time.

Now she's mine.

I know she's scared of commitment. Her family situation growing up makes it hard for her to accept stability. Impermanence is the game she's been playing for too long now.

But I know she cares about me. I know she likes the way I

THE ENFORCER

touch her. Is as turned on by me as I am by her. I plan to prove to her I'm not going anywhere. I'll be as solid as a rock for her until I take my last breath.

She sends secret looks to me as she tunes her electric guitar and checks the mic. She used to acknowledge me before but not like this. Now everything about her says she's here with me.

The band came to the Kremlin this afternoon to practice. Ravil let them use an office on a floor that's mostly empty right now. I sat and watched, unwilling to leave Story alone for even a moment.

"Your boyfriend's making me nervous," Flynn complained at one point, when he kept screwing up his chords. He sent me a lopsided smile, full of carefree charm.

The other two band members had barely said a word, and I realized I probably made them all nervous.

I was about to use the iPad to offer to wait outside, but Story told them, "Get used to it. Oleg's hanging with us now."

And, seemingly as easily as that, I was accepted into the band's sphere. Something that seemed like no more than a fantasy just a few short weeks ago.

Now I'm imagining myself as their roadie, in charge of carrying the heavy equipment and setting it up. Protecting the band. I like the idea.

"We should hire them a manager," Sasha says, also watching. "They're so good. I can't believe they haven't gone bigger."

Maxim nods absently. Like me, he keeps sweeping the club with an alert gaze.

"I mean, I'll do it until we can find someone," Sasha offers.

I stare at her. Without even hesitating this time, I make

149

my expression alive and readable. I lift my brows and spread my hands.

Sasha seems to get it. "I totally would do that for them. I'll be damn good at it, too." She breathes on her nails and pretends to buff them on her sleeve.

"Definitely," Maxim agrees.

I nod.

I do the sign for "thank you." Story spent the past few days making me watch Youtube videos with her to learn the basics. I don't know why I never considered it before.

"You're welcome." Sasha beams. She's already learned most of them, too.

The band picks up their instruments, and Story takes the mic. "Hey everyone, I'm Story Taylor, and we're the Story-tellers. Thank you to Windy City Brew for having us out today."

She doesn't wait for a response, but the band kicks into one of their upbeat numbers. People who weren't paying attention while she was talking now bob their heads in time with the music.

A strange feeling settles over me.

Contentment.

It's like all the pleasure of every time I've seen Story perform condenses into this single moment.

Because now she's mine.

This supernova of a girl belongs to me. Was in my bed last night. Let me tie her up and ravish her all night long.

I check the crowd again, popping my knuckles. The thought of anyone ever trying to hurt her again turns me lethal. But I don't see anything amiss. No one who stands out as not belonging.

My brothers are here watching, as well. They wouldn't let

anything happen to Story, either. I should have trusted them with the details of my ugly past a long time ago.

Story smooths into their next song and then another. The pub is alive now, people happy and talking, people listening. No one's up to dance yet, but that doesn't usually happen until later. The Storytellers have perfected the art of playing just the right groove for the moment, picking things up at the end, when drinks have made the crowd happy and sloppy. Ready to dance.

When the band goes on break, Story beelines for my table and drops into my lap. I band my arm around her waist, feeling as tall as a mountain.

You were great, I type on the iPad.

She twists to kiss me. A long, lingering kiss that probably makes Maxim and Sasha uncomfortable. "I love having you at my shows."

I'm so fucking sorry I missed the last one, I type. I know I let her down, and now that we have the means to communicate, I need to explain myself. *I overslept because of the concussion. I promise, will never miss another one.*

She looks at me for a long time, then she takes my face in both her hands. "I believe you." There's a look of wonder on her face. "That's so scary for me. I think I just expect people to let me down, and then I'm pleasantly surprised when they don't. But with you... I don't know. I could come to..." — she swallows— "depend on you."

Depend on me, I write.

She smiles.

Move in with me, I type.

She freezes, her eyes skittering from the words on the iPad to my face and back.

Blyad'. I pushed it too soon.

I want you in my bed. I try to lighten it up by making it about sex. *Every night.*

It works. She smiles.

"You would terrify all my guitar students."

Oh fuck. Is she actually considering it?

We'll soundproof that empty office for you and the band, I promise. Of course, I'd have to run that by Ravil, but I would do anything to make it happen for her.

She drags her lower lip through her teeth. "Okay."

I was so busy preparing my next offer for how to make this work for her that I barely process what she said.

I raise my eyebrows in disbelief.

She laughs and nods. "Let's try it." She shrugs. "I would love to live with you and the gang."

"What's this?" Maxim interrupts. "Did I hear you're moving in?"

Story shrugs with a big smile. "Well, you do have a great rooftop pool."

Sasha throws back her head and laughs. She points at Story. "You and I are going to raise the roof together at the Kremlin."

Maxim groans, but his expression is indulgent. He's crazy about his wild unruly bride.

Story lifts her glass of water and toasts us all around. "Here's to raising the roof."

STORY

Oleg pushes me up against the side of his Denali, pressing his huge body against mine. His mouth finds my neck, and he bites, insinuating his thigh between my legs for me to grind up.

"Are you going to give it to me rough again?" I ask, breathless.

His large hands cup my ass, and he growls in my ear.

I'm already hot for him—performing makes me horny and so did sitting on his lap between sets. I love the way it feels to get claimed by him.

He hoists my hips up and dry-humps me, the bulge of his cock pressing right against my sweet spot.

"Promise?" I ask.

He chuckles. First chuckle I've ever heard from him.

Then he gently sets me down, opens my door and lifts—not helps—literally *lifts* me inside and onto the seat.

The guy likes to manhandle me.

And I like being manhandled.

He puts the Denali in gear and beeps the horn at Maxim and Sasha, who were waiting in a gorgeous blue Lamborghini to make sure we got out of there safely.

"They want us back next month," I tell Oleg happily. "I was over there collecting our pay and Sasha shows up and introduces herself as our manager."

Oleg steals a glance at me as he drives.

"She basically asked him if he was happy with how we lit the place up and then asked when he'd like to have us back and if he wanted to make it a regular thing. He agreed to have us monthly, and then she asked if he would consider charging a cover and giving it straight to the band."

Oleg looks over at me for more.

"So he says how much is she thinking? She tells him we would start with a five dollar cover, but after we've built our following, she'd bump it to ten."

Oleg tips his head to the side, which I interpret to be his asking what I think.

"I think it's brilliant. He agreed because in the short

term, we're taking the hit. Like we probably won't make as much the first few times, but Sasha said if we start collecting emails from Rue's and then let everyone know where we'll be, we could get the groupies following us everywhere.

Oleg points at his chest.

"You're my groupie?" I ask.

He gives me that ghost of a smile that makes my toes curl in my boots and nods.

"No, you're my bossman. Big Daddy. The guy in charge —in bed, anyway. I twirl a pink lock of hair around my finger and smile at him. I already soaked my panties back in the parking lot when he pushed me up against the vehicle. I can't wait to see what he chooses tonight.

His smile twists into a smirk, transforming his face from dangerous to devastatingly handsome.

He parks at the Kremlin—my new home, I guess, if we're really going through with this thing—and holds my hand until we get into the elevator.

Then he nails me against the elevator wall, kissing the hell out of me, pinning me with his body as his hands ruck my skirt up and tear open my fishnets. I moan when he rubs a finger over my slit, then sinks the tip into my entrance.

The elevator dings, and he lifts me to straddle his waist, carrying me to his bedroom.

I kick off my combat boots. "I should shower," I tell him not because I want to delay the fun, but I probably stink after performing. He catches me around the waist and spanks my ass.

"No showers allowed?" I laugh.

He shakes his head.

"Why not?"

He gives his straining cock a rough squeeze through his

jeans, then points to the bed with a mock-stern lift of his brows.

"You need me in your bed now?"

He doesn't wait to confirm, just hauls me off my feet and swings me around to the bed, where he folds me over and shoves up my skirt.

"Oh my God," I moan, already trembling with excitement. I don't know why I find it so exciting when he gets rough this way, but it doesn't require analysis. It's my thing.

Oleg is my thing.

He smacks my ass. His palm is large and solid, and it propels me forward onto my hands on the bed. I wait, trembling for more.

Oleg is a monster tonight. He tears my fishnets open, and they fall in tatters around my ankles. I don't have panties on underneath them, so I'm bare to him from the waist down. He starts spanking me, fast and hard, like he did my first day here at his place. It hurts but excites me. The pain just filters into pleasure. Into more excitement. The intensity matches the level of Oleg's passion.

Of mine.

My ass burns and tingles, but he still continues, reaching around the front to rub my clit at the same time.

"Oleg, please," I beg, needing more than clitoral stimulation. I want him deep inside me. Showing me his strength and power. Making me feel small and at his mercy.

Cared for.

Protected.

Don't ask me how spanking me makes me feel protected, but it does. My knees are weak with submission. I throw my white flag of surrender at his feet.

Take me, Big Daddy.

Show me what you've got for me.

He delivers one more slap, then I hear his zipper and the rustle of fabric as he steps out of his jeans. I start to crawl up on the bed, but he catches my waist again and drags me back, arranging me in the same position, bent over the bed, my legs spread apart, my bare ass lifted to him.

He lightly slaps between my legs.

I whimper. It didn't hurt, but it's sensitive there —obviously.

He taps my outer thigh, then nudges my feet wider. I obey, spreading my legs even further for him.

He spanks my pussy again.

"Oleg," I whimper.

He strokes his calloused palm down my outer thigh, caressing me. Showing me I'm safe—not that I was worried.

Another quick slap between my legs. I gasp. Then he delivers a series of short, quick slaps that nearly make me come. My pussy is wet and swollen beneath his fingers, making a slick, sticky sound each time he spanks there.

I waggle my ass. "More. Please, Oleg. I need you inside me."

He tugs my skirt, with its elastic waistband, over the top of my head, along with my t-shirt. My bra comes off next. I'm now fully naked for him. He positions me again then growls and drags the head of his cock through my juices. I roll my hips up and push back, desperate for penetration.

He slaps my ass then enters me. I moan in pleasure.

He hums back—my favorite sound.

After a few short thrusts, he pulls out. Gripping my hips, he lifts me up onto my hands and knees on the bed then crawls up behind me and enters again.

"Yes, *please*."

He hums.

Wrapping one hand firmly around the back of my neck,

156

he plows into me in a firm and deliciously disrespectful manner. Just when I don't think it can feel any better, he presses between my shoulderblades, forcing my torso down to the bed in an even more submissive position.

"Oleg," I whimper.

He bucks against me, showing me who's boss with each powerful thrust. His thumb finds my anus, and I squeal in surprise, squeezing against the intrusion.

To my dismay, he pulls out and gives me a few spanks. I hear the sound of the bedside table drawer opening, and then he crawls back behind me and pushes my cheeks wide.

I whimper, suspecting what's going to happen. I both want it and don't want it at the same time.

Or maybe I want it, but I'm embarrassed by the idea.

A little nervous.

It doesn't matter because I know Oleg will take care of me. He'll pay attention to my needs and listen.

I feel a dollop of a cold gel drop over my anus, and I flinch and shiver. Oleg brings his cock to my back entrance.

I hold still, waiting.

Oleg reaches around, rubbing my clit as he applies gentle pressure. After a moment of resisting him, my little ring of muscles relax and open, and he sinks in.

"Oh," I moan. It's intense. Oleg squirts more lube over my crack and rubs it around. When he pushes again it grows even more intense until he gets the head through, then he slips all the way in.

I let out a long vowel on my exhalation.

Oleg goes slowly, taking his time as he fills my ass with his huge cock. All the while, he rubs my clit or finger-fucks me, giving enough attention to my girly-parts to keep me in pleasure.

He hums again.

I hum back.

Oleg works his cock in and out of my ass. My belly flutters with the naughtiness of it. My pussy squeezes on his fingers every time they enter me.

I hear Oleg's breath growing rough. His thrusts take on a little force.

I cry out with the pain/pleasure of it.

He pushes me forward, following until I'm flat on my belly, and he's on top of me, his fingers still under my hips working their magic. He humps my ass in this position, which feels safer—maybe because my flesh isn't as tight this way.

I surrender completely to the sensations. It is total pleasure. There's enough lube, the position's perfect, and the clitoral stimulation has my rocket ready to launch any moment.

"Oleg, oh my God," I moan. "It's so good. So intense. So good." I'm babbling now. I don't care. I don't ever care with Oleg. I'm never self-consciousness. Never self-editing. "Please," I whine. "Pleasepleasepleasepleaseplease."

Oleg's breath grows erratic. His thrusts get harder. He buries three fingers inside my pussy, pushing the heel of his hand over my clit with firm pressure. I squeeze my walls around his fingers, desperate to come.

He grunts and shoves in deep. I feel his thighs shaking against mine as he comes.

I cry out. My pelvic floor muscles don't squeeze—maybe I'm afraid to contract my anus around his dick. Maybe it's just too big. I don't know. It's a different sort of orgasm. Very different, but infinitely more intense.

I shake and shiver beneath him, and it ripples through my body.

He wraps his arms around me and hums softly.

"I love you," I whisper. I haven't said it before, even

though it's been true from the beginning. I was too scared. Too certain things would end, and I'd regret saying it.

But now, I'm moving in. We're taking things forward. I'm still terrified, but I'm trying to trust that Oleg will still be around tomorrow.

That I can count on him to be as solid as he's shown himself to be.

I feel him send the words back to me. Maybe it's not telepathy. Maybe I'm just an empath. It doesn't matter—all that matters is the message.

He loves me.

Oleg loves me, and he's solid as a rock.

I can trust in this. In him.

I can trust in us.

∼

Oleg

I ease out of Story and help her up off the bed and into my bathroom for a couples shower. Washing Story has become my favorite pastime. Right after fucking her. Kissing her. Having her in my bed. Having her in my apartment. Having her as my girlfriend.

I take my time with her, running soapy hands all over her smooth skin, shampooing her hair.

She's tired and can barely stand after the orgasm I gave her, so I hold her up as we go. Towel her dry when we're done. I tuck her into bed and go out to the kitchen to get us a couple glasses of water.

And that's when I see it.

A bottle of Sovetskoye Shampanskoye sitting on the countertop with a red ribbon tied around the neck. I somehow force my fingers to move, to pick up the little card attached.

My name is printed in the bold scrawl I would recognize anywhere.

Skal'pel's handwriting.

Skal'pel's gift.

Soviet champagne was a favorite of mine when I worked for him. It was the first alcohol I'd had to drink as a youth, and I suppose I still bought it out of familiarity. Certainly not out of good taste. I hate the stuff now.

My heart thuds thick and painfully in my chest. My stomach fills with acid.

Skal'pel's here—in Chicago. As I feared, when word got out about me, it also reached him. I'm the loose end that he didn't tie up well enough when he closed up shop.

With trembling fingers, I flip the card. A small photo is taped to the back of the card. It takes me a moment to make it out, but when I do, I almost throw up.

The image is of Sasha and Story in the hot tub on the roof.

Skal'pel' was into games. He would set up tests for me to complete. Testing my loyalty again and again.

I always passed.

Perhaps that's why he let me live.

Many, many times in prison I wished he'd just killed me.

But now? Fuck—*now*?

Story is in my bed. The most beautiful light of my life. The only thing I have worth living for.

Skal'pel' knows about Story. He shot at her from the rooftop, or more likely, had one of his lackey's shoot at her. That fits. The shooter should have known they couldn't hit anyone. The bullets were a warning. A threat. So that when I held this photo in my hand, I would experience real fear for the safety of my beautiful swallow.

My insides turn cold. Swampy. Slimy. Skal'pel's next

move, if I don't answer this message, will be to hurt Story. And it won't be in a typical way. It will be something sick and twisted. Something that would cause me nightmares for the rest of my life. Not that I would live to let it happen to her.

No.

I won't let him near her. Story Taylor must be protected above all else. And that means I have to offer myself up to Skal'pel'. If he wants me dead, he can have me.

He already knows I will sacrifice myself for her. He has no need to make the dark, overt threats. We both know what he's capable of. And he knows me, inside and out.

He knows I would step in front of a bus for the people I love.

But he has no idea the depths of what I'd do for Story.

I leave the bottle on the counter, untouched. I walk quietly back down the dark corridor to my bedroom and open up the drawer in my walk-in closet where I store all the money Ravil's paid me since I started working for him. Other than buying the Denali, I don't spend it. The only activities I have are watching Story play.

I pull out a duffel bag and pack all the stacks of cash into the bag. I get the iPad and open a window with my Swiss bank account—the one Skal'pel' left me somewhere between cutting off my tongue and framing me on drug charges. I make Story the beneficiary, then I compose a message for her.

It's only a couple hours until sunrise. Time enough to lie down beside Story one last time before I go…

CHAPTER 13

*S*tory

The only reason I wake is because I no longer feel Oleg's solid form beside me. I snuggle into the soft sheets, relishing the smell of him that still lingers. After another moment, I crack my eyes and look at the bedside clock. Eleven in the morning. That's pretty normal for me the morning after a gig. I sit up and rub my eyes, looking around.

Oleg doesn't seem to be in the room.

Maybe he went for bagels again.

I swing my legs out of the bed and almost trip over a duffel bag beside it. On top of the navy canvas bag is Oleg's iPad. I smile. He left me a note.

I grab the iPad and wake it up.

STORY,

You are my reason for living, so of course, it is easy to make this choice.

. . .

A COLD CHILL sweeps across my limbs. Renders me limp. My fingers holding the iPad tremble.

MY DEATH IS the best protection for you. Take this money, so I can continue to protect you from the grave.

I love you, my lastochka.

No!

I might have screamed it. Maybe several times.

All I know is that a pounding starts up on the door to the penthouse.

Sobbing, I yank on one of Oleg's t-shirts. The door opens, and Oleg's friends pour in. I don't see them. I barely hear them over the screaming in my head.

Dima picks up the iPad and reads the words out loud to the rest of them.

Someone gathers me into a hug. Nikolai, maybe. I'm passed to Sasha, who also envelopes me against her chest.

I can't stop crying. I only hear snippets of their conversation: *...turning himself in to Skal'pel'...the bottle of Soviet champagne that was delivered here for him... I can't track him, he left his phone here...*

Finally I make myself speak. "S-stop him," I sob. "You have to stop him."

"We will," Ravil answers grimly, even though I can tell by his face he doesn't believe it.

He means he will try.

But we may be too late.

Oh God, we may be too late.

How could this have happened? How did I fall in love for

the first time in my life only to lose him in the matter of two weeks?

I'm hyperventilating. It's that ugly, out of control sobbing where you can't breathe. Can't speak. Can't release the torrent of emotion trapped in your body.

"Why?" I sob, even though he told me why.

He did it for me.

He sacrificed his life, so I would stay safe.

I hate myself now for insisting on going to gigs. Making him worry about my safety.

Fuck, if I would've know it meant him turning himself in to get butchered by some cruel doctor, I would've holed up here in this penthouse with him for the rest of my life.

The salt in my tears burns my eyes.

Someone hands me a tissue. Then another.

Then the whole box.

I can't stop the hurricane.

"You have to stop him," I repeat again. "Please."

Some of the men have left the room. I'm not sure what's happening.

"Are you going to find him?" I ask. I'm like a lost child in the airport. I don't even know where to begin or who to turn to.

Ravil comes to me. "We're trying to track them down. I'll be honest. It might be difficult. Skal'pel' is a smart man who could be using any identity and wearing any face. He could've been living anywhere. But Dima's working every angle we can think of."

I shake my head, refusing to accept that answer. "No. You have to find him. You have to get there before anything happens. How long has he been gone? Does anyone know?"

"Not yet," Ravil murmurs, pulling out his phone. "But I'll

check with Maykl down at the front door. We have security footage."

I stumble around the room, my stomach scrunched up under my ribs. "This is wrong," I mutter between hiccuping sobs. "It's all wrong."

"Story." Ravil gently grips my shoulder. "I'd like you to stay here while we figure this out, okay? You may still be in danger, and I need to keep you safe."

I blink at him then burst into fresh tears, but I nod. "Yes," I say. I want to be with them. I need to be with the people who know and love Oleg.

Because I need them to bring him back.

~

Oleg

I blink, trying to open my eyes, but even when I do, I can't see. I shift. My wrists are bound. There must be a bag over my head.

I'm still alive.

I'm surprised by that fact.

At dawn, I walked outside the Kremlin and stood outside the building to wait.

I stood motionless for three hours, and then a black limo pulled up across the street and parked. When no one got out, I waited a few minutes, then crossed the street and opened the door to the back seat.

It was empty.

"Get in," the driver said, without looking back at me. He was American. Possibly a thug for hire. He drove to a private airstrip and parked. There, the back doors were simultaneously opened by two more thugs—also American—who told me to get out and get on the plane—a small jet parked on the tarmac. I walked up the steps. The moment I arrived at the top, someone stabbed a needle into my neck. I didn't fight them or the drug. I just looked around for Skal'pel' before I topped into the waiting arms of the two thugs who'd followed me in.

I never saw him.

He may never have been in Chicago at all.

That fit. He wouldn't risk his own neck to get me.

I test my bonds. My wrists are bound in front with what feels like zip ties. I'm sitting upright in a comfortable seat—the jet's chair, maybe?

"You're awake." The mild-mannered voice of my former boss reaches my ears. He's speaking in Russian.

The bag comes off. We are on the jet—at least, I think it's the same jet, but it may be a different one. Skal'pel' sits across from me in an expensive tailored suit. I don't recognize his face—he's changed it. But I would remember the voice anywhere. And his body frame hasn't changed, other than a few extra pounds.

I don't move. I have no fight in me. My only plan was to surrender to this man to save Story.

"I appreciate the way you operate, Oleg."

The routine is familiar. The fond way he looks at me. The praise. Then he'll tell me what he wants with a total and complete expectation that I will deliver.

And I always did.

He leans forward and pulls my lower eyelid down, like he's inspecting my pupil. "Are you all there? All the way back?"

I don't answer.

"Oleg?" That quiet, expecting tone coaxes a nod out of me before I realize I'm giving it.

He lifts a finger, and a thin guy with a mustache appears

with a bottle of water, which he opens and hands to Skal'pel'. My former employer leans forward and brings the bottle to my lips.

I don't want to accept his help, but the moment the water enters my mouth, I swallow greedily. The tranquilizer made me cotton-mouthed and thirsty.

"You did the right thing. Your little songbird will be safe. No more bullets on the rooftop."

Fuck. That was him. I guess I knew deep down it had to be.

I don't move. If this were a movie, I would struggle against my bonds. Lunge out like I wanted to kill him for talking about hurting my girl. But it's not a movie. I hang on his every word, needing to hear the rest of them.

I've been waiting twelve years for closure. To know why he abandoned me. Balled me up like a used rag and then lit me on fire and left me to burn.

"I never knew what sort of woman would turn your head, but I knew she'd have to be unusual. It's personality for you, isn't it? Not that your Story isn't lovely. But you never looked twice at normal beauty. You were unmoved by the perfect tits or a nice pair of long legs. It takes a special one to captivate you."

I scowl.

"I'm sorry, Oleg." Skal'pel' considers me. "You were never anything but loyal to me. You always did what I asked. Performed better than any man I've hired since. But your size made you too hard to hide." He offers me another drink, and I take it. "Changing your face wouldn't have worked. And keeping you with me would've been a tell for my old identity. I had to cut you loose and ensure no one would come after you."

God help me, it's all I can do to keep the skepticism from my expression.

"I left you money. Enough to make you a rich man when you got out." His expression turns to disappointment, like I'm the one who let him down. "You never used it. Just a few thousand dollars to get to America."

I shrug.

"The rest of it is still sitting in a bank in your name. Untouched."

I don't respond.

He gets up and starts pacing, hands clasped behind his back.

I turn and check out who's on the plane. I see the two men in the back who put me on the plane. A third, skinny, more secretarial-looking guy with a mustache. He's the one who brought the water.

The door to the pilot's cabin is closed.

Skal'pel' goes on with his monologue. My being mute now hardly makes a difference. The man always preferred to hear himself talk. Not like Ravil, who listens.

But he's just as smart as Ravil. He strategizes just as well. He reads and understands people like Ravil does. At least, I always felt like he knew me better than I knew myself. That's what makes him a master manipulator.

"You joined the bratva. A surprising choice although perhaps not, considering the friends you'd made in prison."

I'm sickened by how closely he followed my life after he mutilated my body and ruined my life. I don't know what I'd thought he would do. I hadn't wanted to think about him. What had become of him. Where he was or what he was doing.

But I certainly never imagined he was tracking and following me. My life.

It turns my stomach.

Or maybe that's just the aftereffects of the tranquilizer.

"I realized that my gift to you wasn't the consolation I'd hoped it would be. You didn't crave cash. You craved a master to serve. And you found one with your new bratva cell. Ravil Baranov, smuggler and self-made real estate mogul of downtown Chicago."

Now I want to kill him.

It's all I can do not to flex my hands against the zip ties. I don't like him talking about Ravil. And I especially don't like his assessment of me, however true it may be.

I could snap his neck. Right here, right now. He's within my reach. But I might get shot in the back of the head before I finished the job. Would it be worth it?

The world would be safe from this maniac.

Story would be safe.

Oh fuck, *Story.*

Just thinking of her brings on a wave of grief so heavy it nearly drowns me.

I left her. My sweet *lastochka.*

And probably like Skal'pel's payment to me, that bag of cash I bequeathed to her won't be any kind of consolation for my death. She doesn't seem to care much about money, anyway.

I didn't think this through. I just blindly followed the path Skal'pel' laid for me, just like I always have. I'd thought I was doing this for Story. Sacrificing myself, so she could live. Being the honorable, trustworthy man I've always considered myself to be.

But this isn't honoring Story. And sure as hell isn't honoring myself. This is the first time in my life I really have something worth living for, and I chose not to fight for it?

Not to even try to find a solution other than the one Skal'pel' picked for me?

Am I really going to let him continue to write the script of my life?

"I don't know who figured out your connection with me, but when I saw a reward had been put up for your safe capture, I had to come for you." Now he turns an indulgent gaze on me. Like I'm the wayward child he's taking back into his fold, instead of the psychopath who thought cutting out my tongue and putting me in prison was the best way to reward me for my loyal service.

"I couldn't let them capture you, even though you probably hold little knowledge of value in that glorious, big head of yours." He drops back into his seat and crosses one ankle over his knee.

"I could have just sent an executioner." He stands again to pace away from me. "It would've been safer for me. Far easier. Definitely simpler." He turns and looks at me. "But the truth is, I've missed your service, Oleg." He flicks a glance at the American thugs. "No one takes care of business the way you used to. Without complaint or interjections. You never did speak much, even when you had a tongue."

He paces back. "So I came myself for you. And your obedient response to my message showed me you're still as reliable as ever." He passes by me and places a hand on my shoulder in the way he used to show his approval or affection. He squeezes.

One blow with both my fists would knock him out.

"Again, I couldn't bring myself to kill you. I'd rather have you by my side again, where you belong. Serving your old master." He's behind me now, where I can't see him.

Where he can't see my face.

I make a few micromovements of discovery. My ankles

aren't bound. I'm not tied to this seat. And that's when I remember—you can't fire a gun on an airplane.

Those thugs would know that, too.

"Would you like to serve me again, Oleg?"

I wait for him to walk around to the front of me. He's holding a syringe. A fatal dose of poison if I answer incorrectly? It doesn't matter. People always underestimate how quickly I can move for my size. I lunge out of my chair and twist his head around on his neck, snapping it. I take the syringe from his hand as he falls.

My movements are slower than I'd like—the after-effects of the drug still weigh me down, but I have far too much practice in clearing a room for it to stop me.

The thugs in the back come for me, guns drawn. They won't fire them, not unless they want us all to die.

I plunge the syringe into the first guy's neck and dodge a blow from the second one, knocking into his belly with my elbow. I punch him again with an awkward side-swing of both arms, but I put enough power behind it to lift him off his feet and knock the wind out of him.

A blow to the face, and he goes down. The mustached man picks up a gun from one of the fallen men and points it at me, his hand trembling.

I shake my head.

"Don't move, or I'll shoot."

I risk it. I take two long steps to reach him, snatch the gun from his hand and strike him in the temple with it. He goes down.

I search the pockets of the thugs and find the zip ties, then fasten them around the wrists of the three guys still breathing. Killing them might be cleaner, but I can make that call later.

Now I have to get this plane turned around.

CHAPTER 14

S *tory*

I don't know how many hours it is before Ravil gets a text from an unknown number, but it comes. There's a wild scramble of activity.

Oleg's alive. On a plane flying back to Chicago.

I cry more tears—this time of relief. And then there's more waiting.

As I wait, my grief morphs into anxiety. A gnawing, itching anxiety. The kind that's plagued me my whole life. I consider it to be my gut instinct telling me when something's not right.

When it's time to bail.

And the longer the minutes stretch until Oleg is back, the stronger the feeling grows.

I get bundled into the back of Oleg's Denali with Nikolai and Dima in front, and we leave, along with two other vehicles, for some private airstrip I've never heard of.

It's snowing. Thick, wet flakes that hit the windshield and melt the minute they touch it. Nikolai drives. Dima brings a laptop along and is searching things as we drive, making short comments to his brother in Russian, then pausing to throw an apologetic smile over his shoulder at me.

The nervous buzzing grows louder, so I can't think about anything. I can't remember if I've eaten anything today. I don't think I have. My lips are dry, my throat is parched.

Vaguely, I realize I have to perform tonight at Rue's. It seems like last night's performance was a lifetime ago.

When we get there, Nikolai turns around and says, "I'm going to need you to wait in the Denali, okay? Please don't come out, or you'll be an accessory to anything you see out there. Understand?"

I think I nod. I'm not sure. My brain is barely functioning.

And then I'm alone in the vehicle. I should be excited. I get to see Oleg. I thought he was dead, but he's coming back to me.

Except it's clear as day that there is no going "back."

I'll never feel the way I did last night again.

That moment has passed, and we are on to a new one. And in this one, I don't even want to be here.

Sitting in the warmed seats, watching the sleet fall, I feel like I'm waiting for something awful to happen.

But what?

Is it Oleg coming back?

No.

It's me breaking up with him.

That's the gnawing anxiety. I know this isn't right. I can't do this thing with him.

~

Oleg

We land back at the same airstrip we took off from. I was

able to communicate my desires to the pilot, who thinks I'm going to kill him.

He's a talker. I sit in the co-pilot's seat for the duration of the trip, and he's one constant stream of monologue, nervous sweat dripping from his forehead.

I left the phone on speaker, so Maxim could hear everything, since he'll have to fix this.

The pilot already told us he didn't know Skal'pel' very well but flew him in from Florida, and that's where he had orders to fly back. He had enough fuel to turn the plane around and got clearance to land back in Chicago.

He says he doesn't want to know what happened in the cabin of the plane, and as far as he's concerned, it's none of his business. Then he talked a lot about his wife and two small kids. How they're expecting him home this afternoon, and he's their only income.

After he lands the plane, Maxim lets him off the hook.

"Here's what's going to happen," he tells him. "You're going to stay in that cockpit until we've dealt with whatever went down in the cabin. Then I'm going to let you know it's time to come out, we'll pay you for your time, and you can go home to Sarah Jean and your sweet kids, Thomas and Flora on Andaluz Lane."

The pilot draws a sharp breath at hearing that Maxim already knows his family's details.

"You flew this plane for Dr. Armor—is that what you said his name was?"

"Yes, D-Dr. Armor," the pilot stammers.

"Dr. Armor changed his mind about going back to the Florida Keys and asked you to turn the plane around. When you got here, he got off and told you he was staying for a while and wouldn't need your services. He asked you to take a commercial flight back home. That was the last you heard from him. Understand?"

"Got it," the pilot says quickly. "Absolutely."

"You never saw anyone else on the plane."

"Never."

"Okay, stay where you are. If you move before I come for you, our arrangement will need to be reworked. Are we clear?"

"Crystal."

The pilot shoots me a quick, frightened look.

"Oleg, we're outside. Let us in."

I go to the cabin to open the doors, and my brothers come in. Maxim does a quick sweep of the place, assessing, then gives orders. Pavel and Adrian get Skal'pel's body out. Maxim and Ravil question the two thugs who are conscious. Like the pilot, they claim to know very little about Dr. Armor or his business, other than being his personal bodyguards.

"Story's waiting in your Denali," Nikolai says, handing me the keys.

"Go ahead," Ravil says. "We'll take care of this."

I'm not a demonstrative guy. I don't try to communicate often. But I stop and clasp the hand of each of my brothers and look into their eyes to show them how much it means to me that they have my back.

They are my family. I held myself back from them these last two years because of the wounds inflicted by Skal'pel'. The emotional ones, not the physical. But I'm done with that. I won't give my loyalty where it isn't deserved again. My future is with Story, and my family is here with me now.

"*Mudak*," Dima mutters when I clasp his hand. "Story was out of her mind with grief. You may not give a shit about your life, but the rest of us do."

I circle my fist over my chest in the sign I learned for

sorry.

"Yeah, you better go tell that to your girl." He tips his head in the direction of the tarmac.

I climb down the stairs and jog to the vehicle. Story looks small and lost in the back seat.

Lonely.

I throw the door open and gather her up. She clings like a koala, wrapping her legs around my waist, her arms around my neck. She makes a broken whimpering sound, but she doesn't speak.

Story, my beautiful lastochka.

She still says nothing and won't loosen her grip on my neck, so I can see her face. I just hold her, breathing in her sweet scent, kissing her neck. Still, she says nothing. We're getting soaked in the sleet, so I walk around to put her in the front seat, passenger side where I can see her face.

There's so much pain in her gaze. Almost like it hurts her to look at me.

It slices a gash right across my chest. I put that pain there. I hurt her—the one person I was trying so hard to protect.

How could I have done this?

I sign *sorry,* but she looks away, blinking back tears.

I cup her face and bring my forehead to hers. She doesn't move. I try the sign again.

She swallows. "I'm glad you're alive." Her voice is choked.

Sorry, I sign again. It's all I really know how to say. I see Dima left my iPad on the driver's seat for me, but I don't pick it up. Even if I could speak, I wouldn't have the words. I don't even know how to navigate when Story's clammed up, herself.

I guess I'm getting a taste of my own medicine, and it's a fucking bitter one.

Story pulls her legs into the vehicle and pushes me away. "You're getting wet," she says.

Fuck.

I shut the door, walk around to the driver's side, and get in, picking up the iPad to at least try. *Dima called me an asshole for what I did. I'm sorry I caused so much grief.*

Story shakes her head. "You weren't an asshole." Her voice sounds so fucking heavy. Exhausted. She reaches out and squeezes my forearm. "You were being you. Trying to protect me and do it all by yourself without reaching out for help from anyone else."

Her words strike home.

I nod. *Da.* She's right. I could have played it so differently. I could have gone to Ravil, and he and Maxim would've come up with a better option. But instead I played straight into Skal'pel's fucking plan for me. Forsaking Story and my brothers in my effort to protect them.

"Oleg... did you go to him to die?"

I suck in a breath and nod.

She sags and looks away from me, out the window.

Fuck, I'm losing her. Frantic, I type on the iPad. *I went to die, but as soon I arrived, I realized I'd made the wrong choice. It wasn't right to sacrifice myself and surrender, it was time to fight.*

For you.

She gives me a searching look then looks straight ahead at the jet on the tarmac. "I have to play at Rue's tonight."

Gospodi. I forgot. It's Saturday night.

I start the Denali up and put it in gear, turning it around. I don't know where the fuck we are, so I turn on the map function on my phone to get us back, checking the clock. Enough time to get home and get Story's guitar from the Kremlin before we head over.

178

I point at Story and give the sign for *hungry*, raising my brows, the way we learned.

"Am I hungry? Yeah, actually I could eat. You?"

I nod. We hit the first drive-thru we see—a Wendy's. I use the iPad to order, which makes Story laugh, lightening the mood a little.

We eat as I drive, and then she drops the bomb on me.

"Oleg, I can't move in with you."

Somehow I keep the Denali from crashing into the guy in front of me.

She doesn't go on, which makes it a million times worse.

I make the sign for *why?* by pulsing my middle finger by my forehead, brows down.

"I thought I could do this. I care about you. I really do. But I have so much drama in my life already. And your life is really intense. I mean, you're in the Russian *mafiya*, and you're getting shot at, and I'm getting shot at, and then I thought you were going to die, and it's just too much."

I want to argue with her. I reach for the iPad, but realize I can't type and drive at the same time.

Fuck.

I pick up her hand instead and shake my head.

She pulls away, gutting me. "I *can't*. I need you to accept this. Please don't make this harder than it already is."

Blyad'. I grip the steering wheel. Part of me refuses to believe it. I want to fight for her. But she just asked me not to, and I'm also not the guy who doesn't understand *no* means *no*.

Story wants me out of her life.

The irony is too thick to swallow. I chose to live and fight because of her, and I lost her anyway.

I'd almost rather be dead.

CHAPTER 15

*S*_{tory}

I asked Oleg to drop me at Rue's. I told him not to come in.

He honored my request.

I was half-afraid he wouldn't. I mean, I know the guy's stubborn. Dogmatic in his devotion to me.

Somehow I made it through the night. I actually don't think anyone even noticed anything was off with me, which made it all the worse.

Because that anxiety that was brewing, the sense of everything being wrong—it didn't go away when I broke up with Oleg.

In fact, it got worse.

Now, as I stand outside Rue's to catch an Uber home, I practically want to crawl out of my own skin. The buzzing in my ears isn't just from the amps. It's noise. Noise that makes it impossible to think through the slightest problem, like how to open the app and check for my ride.

A familiar white Denali pulls up in front of me.

Oleg.

Tears instantly pop into my eyes. Of course he's still here. He probably sat in the parking lot for the entire show, waiting to make sure I got home safely.

I pull open the door. "You can't be here!" Tears clog my throat.

"Let me take you home," the Australian-accented voice from the iPad says.

My shoulders sag. "I called an Uber." I already know I'm going to get in the Denali.

Oleg is my ride, even if I don't want him to be.

He rubs an open hand over his head. *Please.*

I blink back the tears. "Fine." I get in. "But this is it. This is our goodbye. Please don't come back here again."

He nods his agreement.

Except when we get to my place, he parks and opens his door.

I want to protest, but I don't. Maybe part of me wants to drag out our goodbye, too. He carries my guitar and walks me to the door, taking my keys from me to open the front door then following me up the stairs.

He unlocks the door to my apartment and pushes it open.

And then he's on me. His arm bands behind my back, his lips descend over mine with a bruising force.

I surrender. Completely.

I'm the girl who lives in the moment, and this is our moment.

I give him my tongue, loop my arms behind his neck, standing on my tiptoes to reach. He grips my ass, yanking my body up against his as he claims my mouth.

He backs me against the arm of the sofa and picks my leg up behind the knee to spread me open for him.

"Oleg."

He cups my mons firmly, the warmth of his fingers

searing through my panties. He slides his fingers beneath the fabric, rubbing over my entrance as our lips tangle. He sucks my lower lip and dips a finger inside me.

I reach for his jeans, opening them, desperate to get him inside me. He drags his mouth down my neck and nips me as I get his cock out and positioned at my entrance.

I teeter backward, my hips balanced on the stuffed arm of the sofa, but he loops a strong arm behind my back to hold me in place, at the same time he yanks my hips forward toward his.

Pushing the gusset of my panties to the side, he enters me, and we're moving together from the first moment he's inside.

We fuck like our lives depend on it.

We're the last humans on Earth. It's the last chance we'll ever have for sex. We have to make it count for all of humanity.

He fucks me hard, thrusting in and up. Each stroke feels necessary. Satisfying. Life-affirming.

I cling to him, one hand around his neck to keep me suspended, my knees spread wide for his plunder. I love his wild passion. The way, once he starts, it's like he can't hold back with me. Like making me come is his life's only pursuit.

Time suspends. Pleasure shimmers all around us, building, aching. Climbing.

I don't even realize tears are leaking from my eyes. I'm not sad. It's just necessary. The intensity meets the burning flame in my soul. My reason for living.

I'm unusually quiet. Other than that single utterance of his name when we began, I don't beg, don't moan, don't cry out. It's like this is too serious an occasion for the usual passion-chatter. Too significant. The heavy rasping of our breaths is the only music we dance to.

There's no question we will climax as one. I feel the surge

of his orgasm, and my own rises to meet it. He's the first one to make a sound. An urgent vocalization. I return the call.

And then we both come. He arcs in deep and stays, shooting his wad. I suck on his neck, my internal muscles contracting around his cock, milking it for more. It goes on and on. A completion, not just of sex, but of us. Of our relationship.

One last momentous time together to remember each other by.

Oleg eases out of me and helps me back to my feet. Dark concern swirls in his brown eyes.

I put my hand on his face, memorizing his beloved features. "I love you." It's worth saying, even if we're breaking up. And I say it as an ending. An *Amen* to the sacred space we gave to each other.

And Oleg does seem to understand we're still breaking up because the words make his forehead crinkle as if he's in pain.

My anxiety revs back up, starting to eat away at the endorphins released by the incredible sex.

I need to end this thing. Maybe that's why I'm still anxious. Because he's still here. It's still going.

"Goodbye, Oleg," I say firmly.

He flinches, visibly destroyed by my words.

I feel equally destroyed. I don't know why the anxiety isn't getting better.

He cups the back of my head and presses his lips to mine. This time the kiss isn't brutal, it's soft and sweet.

And then he turns and leaves without looking at me again.

I thought I'd cried all my tears out earlier thinking Oleg was dead, but it seems I still have an ocean left to cry. I mean to walk myself to the shower and put myself to bed, but instead I find myself on my knees, wracked with sobs.

~

Oleg

I don't get out of bed other than to eat a little the next day. Or the day after.

Not even on the third day.

I can't face what I lost. I had Story. She was mine for two short weeks. She let me hold her. Make love to her. Bring her home.

She was going to move in with me. For the first time in years, I had a reason to get up in the morning. Things felt possible again. I was willing to stretch myself. Start interacting with my environment. Join the living.

There was such a lightness around me. I didn't hate my body for betraying me. I found new ways to communicate. But most importantly, I got to be around Story. My obsession. I had her to myself—all her minutes. All her hours. She sang and played her guitar in my bed. Stood in my shower. Let me love her.

Loved me back.

She said so.

But she didn't choose us. She didn't choose me. I caused her too much stress, and she opted out. I can't blame her. Not for a second. I want to punch myself in my own face for hurting her. For making her cry. For causing her more trauma.

Wednesday morning, Nikolai and Dima come into my room without knocking. I'm on my back in the center of the bed. "So what the fuck happened?" Nikolai demands.

I ignore him, staring at the ceiling.

"This place stinks. You have to get up and take a shower, *mudak*. And come out and eat something."

I keep ignoring him.

"I'm guessing Story broke up with you?"

185

I sit up, my hands curling into fists. I'm suddenly overwhelmed with the urge to punch my brothers—something I've never done.

Nikolai and Dima seem to realize it because they step back in unison. "I'm sorry." Nikolai holds his hands up. They both know my fists are as lethal as any gun.

"I do not want to fuck with you, Oleg," Nikolai says. "We just want to maybe talk it through. See if we can help."

I shake my head. There is no help. Not for me and Story.

Despite my refusal of their offer to assist, they both sit down on the foot of the bed.

Now I really want to kill them.

"What scared her?" Dima asks. "The danger?"

I glare at him. He tosses the iPad over to me.

I growl, but suddenly the need to discuss Story becomes a fresh addiction. Like talking about her will bring here back.

The drama, I type.

Nikolai cocks his head. "Hmm." He sounds doubtful, like he's questioning my answer.

"Of course you know her way better than I do, but I'm not sure that fits. I mean, if she couldn't handle the drama, she would've called the cops the minute she found you shot in the back of her van, right?"

"*Da.* To me, it almost seems the opposite," Dima agrees. "What did she tell Sasha? She has a high tolerance for chaos. She didn't even freak over getting shot at on the roof. I mean, the girl can really *roll* with things." He says it appreciatively, and I'm partly pleased and partly infuriated with his admiration.

Panic starts to shiver deep in the pit of my stomach. Do I not even understand why she left me? Was it really *me* she couldn't handle?

Nikolai seems to guess at my fear because he says,

"There's no question she loves you. I haven't seen anyone that torn apart as when she thought you'd gone to your death."

"Maybe Maxim when he thought Sasha was dead," Dima counters, "But yeah. She was a hot mess."

A hot mess.

"So, to me, it seems more like it was about you leaving. She absorbed all the rest of the crazy shit that went down without much of a complaint," Nikolai says.

Me leaving. That strikes a chord somewhere.

Story had told me she couldn't rely on the people in her life. That she'd had a lot of love from her family but no stability.

That must be why she said she always left relationships. Maybe she's the type who leaves before she gets close. Before she can be abandoned or let down again.

She'd liked that I was steady. I showed up week after week. She could count on me.

And so by leaving, I did the one thing she was afraid of. I proved myself unreliable. As capable of wounding her as the other people closest to her.

I betrayed Story. Abandoned her.

Fuck.

I didn't just poke her wound, I stabbed her in it. After she'd told me how scary it was to rely on someone.

Gospodi.

I thought I'd turned myself into Skal'pel' for her and left her money for a new start, but was it any kind of gift worth receiving? A bag of cash and another abandonment?

It was no gift at all. Story's the type who'd rather risk her own life and stay by my side. She'd already proven that to me. And I made her sacrifice mean nothing.

"What?" Nikolai demands.

I type, *I abandoned her when she needed me to be her rock.*

"Fuuuuuuck," Dima says after he reads it.

"So you have to show her that you're still her rock," Nikolai advises.

I hold my hands out to ask *how?*

"Tell her. Keep going to her show. I wouldn't get in her face too much—you don't want to disrespect her wishes—but prove you're not going anywhere. Not ever again. And communicate. I seriously feel like shit that we didn't get to know you until Story moves in. I don't know why we didn't try harder to draw you out of your shell. I mean, fuck. We could've learned sign language a long time ago."

"Definitely," Dima concurs. "Hell, maybe we could even get you a speech therapist. I've been doing some research, and it sounds like they could teach you new ways to talk."

I want to weep with gratitude at the flicker of hope the twins sparked—not about talking but about winning back Story. I stand, and when the twins also stand, I pull them in for a handshake and man-hug, thumping them each on the back.

"Oh. Okay. Wow. You must feel better," Dima says, chuckling. "How can I help?"

I shake my head. I already know what I'm going to do. And it's going to work. It may be a long game, but I'm willing to play it.

I'll play it until the day I die if I have to.

I'm Story's rock, and she's going to know it and believe it and feel it right down into her bones.

I love her, and I will never abandon her again.

CHAPTER 16

*S**tory*

"Story? Hey, it's Mom."

The warning bells all go off at once at the sound of my mom's voice. It radiates with the heaviness of depression.

"Mom, are you okay?"

"Uh… I've been better. Sam and I broke up."

Tears spear my eyes, not for my mom but my own self-pity kicking into gear. Like, seriously? Do I have to deal with my mom's breakup right now when I haven't even managed my own yet?

"Can you come over? I don't want to be alone."

Blinking back tears, I shove my feet into my boots and pick up my keys. "Okay, Mom. I'll come right now. Are you at home?"

"Um… yeah. I'm at home." She sounds lost.

I have to breathe through the spike of fear that accompanies all of my mom's episodes. The fact that she reached out is good. Getting her help early prevents the really damaging lows. "I'm heading over now."

"Thanks, hon," my mom says, sounding like she's lost in a dream. I know the feeling.

I get in my car and head over to her place, numbness taking over the anxiety.

I've been anxious ever since Oleg left my place Saturday night. In fact, every day that's passed, it's grown stronger and stronger.

It doesn't make sense. Usually when I get that anxious feeling, I cut ties with whomever I'm getting too close to, and it immediately drops away. I consider it my gut instinct for when it's time to move on. My relationship compass.

And I had it with Oleg. I had it so strongly Saturday.

And yet breaking up didn't ease the sense of dread in the pit of my stomach.

And now I have this shit with my mom. Like the Universe decided that I didn't have enough drama in my life with the whole Oleg sacrificing himself to an evil doctor and nearly getting killed and then our breakup.

I turn my phone on to call my sister Dahlia to let her know what's going on with Mom.

"Hey sis, what's up?" she answers cheerily.

"Eh." It's all I can manage. I suddenly feel like I can't do this.

"What is it, Story? Is it Mom?"

I sniff. "Yeah. Sort of."

I don't know why I said *sort of*. I wasn't calling to talk about my problems.

"Is she okay?" I hear the alarm in Dahlia's voice, which I understand. We're all dreading that call. The one where we find out Mom is suicidal.

"Yeah, I think so. She sounded depressed, so I'm heading over there. I'll make sure she has an appointment with her counselor."

"Good. I'm glad she recognizes when she needs help," Dahlia says.

"I know." I get choked up again.

"Are you okay? Do you need me to come home?"

"No, no. I'm okay. I just, um, I'm having a hard time right now, too."

"Oh no! What's happening?"

Tears start streaming down my face. I take my hand off the wheel to swipe at them with my fingers. "Remember that guy I told you about?"

"Oh my gosh, yes! What's going on?"

"Dahlia, I think I might be messed up."

"What do you mean?"

"I don't know. Like I'm broken. Maybe I got Mom's relationship gene."

"Definitely not," my sister says firmly. "What's going on? You really liked this guy, right?"

"I did," I wail. "But then I got that anxious feeling that I usually get. You know—the sign. That's when I know things aren't going to work, and I should get out. Only I broke things off with him, and the agitation's only growing."

"Okay, wait a minute. So you think it's a sign when you get anxious in a relationship, and it means you need to break it off?"

"Yeah. Like it's my gut telling me things aren't going to work, and I should stop before things get too deep."

"Wait, wait, wait. That's why you never date anyone for more than a couple months?"

"Yes, but the thing is, this time it didn't work. I'm still anxious. And now I'm totally confused."

"Story, did you ever stop to consider that anxiety isn't instinct, it's fear?"

That lands like a missile between my eyes.

I can't even answer.

"What if the anxiety is because you're afraid to get too close to someone not an intuition that it's not going to work out?"

Huh. My tears stop falling. That feels *right.*

Like it could be true.

"So you pushed this guy away, and now you're scared because you think you lost him."

"I don't know…"

"Maybe you do know."

I laugh in spite of myself. "You think you're so wise just because you're the only one in the family who's kept a relationship more than three years."

"Well, Mom and Dad did. But they did it so badly it made all the rest of us think relationships are impossible."

"You didn't."

"That's because I had Joe."

"Yep. Joe's the best," I agree, my heart suddenly aching with longing for Oleg.

Oleg is a hundred times better than Joe, in my opinion. Oleg is the perfect man.

What if I *am* anxious because I lost him not because I was supposed to leave him?

What if he's my Joe? The one.

My forever-after?

I pull up in front of my mom's apartment and park. She's waiting on the front step, despite the cold.

"Hey, Mom." I pull her into a hug.

"I kicked him out," she says, bursting into tears. "And now… I think I want him back."

I cry with her. "I did the same thing, Mom. And I think it was a mistake."

~

Oleg

Saturday night, I shower and put on a clean shirt and jeans. I shave my face and use some of Maxim's aftershave, and then I drive to Rue's.

Wednesday I mailed a hand-written letter to Story. It took me forever because I typed into the iPad first to make sure I spelled the English right, but I wanted it to be hand-written not printed or emailed. It said,

Story,

My beautiful lastochka.

I failed you. I thought I was doing the right thing by leaving for your safety, but I realize now that you never wanted to be safe. You wanted to be able to depend on me. And by abandoning you, I proved myself undependable.

I want you to know I respect your wish to end our relationship, but you are my life's purpose.

Being your rock.

Keeping you safe.

Watching you perform.

These are the things I live and breathe for.

So I'm not going to stop coming to your shows. I won't stop ensuring you get home safely. I'll be there for you in any way you want me. To catch you when you dive off the stage or to carry in your equipment or just to sit in the corner and never make contact again.

You can depend on me.

I fucked up, but I won't do it again. Not ever.

I'm your rock. You can rely on me.

I promise.

Ya lyublyu tebya. *I love you.*

Oleg

She didn't call or text after getting it. Hell, I don't know if she even read it. Maybe she just threw the thing in the trash. Not because she despises me—I don't think that's the case. But because it was too painful for her.

She's trying to make a clean break.

That's the biggest weight that hangs over my head as I park in the lot behind Rue's Lounge. I didn't come early enough to get my table because I didn't want to piss Story off. I didn't want to fluster her before her performance or make her think she had to talk to me.

I slip in now after she's started her first set. The place is hopping. The Storytellers are rocking the Jane's Addiction song, "Jane Says." Story's hair is back to platinum blonde, and she's wearing a dark shade of lipstick that makes her eyes pop.

I slip in and stand against the back wall. I hope when she sees me, she doesn't ask me to leave. I pray she's read the letter and understands that I have to be here. I have to prove to her I am the man she believed me to be.

Annie, one of the cocktail waitresses, brings me a beer without my asking.

Story slips into one of her original songs and then another. Their performance is flawless, and yet I see the wear of the week on her. She doesn't smile or bounce as much. She's just smooth and professional.

And then she sees me. Her gaze lands on me and sticks, but she doesn't falter singing the words or strumming her chords.

She expected me.

So she read my letter.

She finishes her song and paces the front of the stage.

"Hey. I've been working on a new song, do you want to hear it?"

I clap my hands as the crowd cheers.

"It's about this guy. You probably know him. He usually sits right there." She points at my table where some other assholes are sitting tonight.

I go still.

"I let him into my life recently, and it was good. Really good. But sometimes we run from things in our life that are good. Because having them would give us something worth losing, you know?"

She shoots a pained look my way, and people turn to see who she's looking at.

There he is. That's the guy she climbs, I hear the regulars saying.

"But the real heroes are the ones who keep showing up. Even when you push them away. And that's what Oleg does for me. He's as solid as they come. And this song is for him."

Story puts the microphone in the stand and positions herself in front of it, legs wide.

I KNOW YOU FROM A DISTANCE / I haven't had a taste.
Didn't want to let you / cuz I only like the chase.
You are in my sphere / I am in your ear,
Then you take me home, but you won't come in.
I don't know, I don't know, I don't know what I'm doing,
But when I'm with you / when I'm with you-ou.
I don't need anything. I don't need anything at all.
I'm up against the wall / your hands tangle in my clothes
I'm kissing, I'm biting, I'm rocked down to my toes
When you show up, you show up strong.
I don't know, I don't know, I don't know what I'm doing,

But when I'm with you / when I'm with you-ou.
I don't need anything. I don't need anything at all.
Set the house on fire, burn it to the ground.
The cities fall, wreckage all around
When you show up, you show up strong
I don't know, I don't know, I don't know what I'm doing,
but I'm with you / when I'm with you-ou,
I don't need anything at all.
And I don't know, I don't know, I don't know what we're doing.
But I don't need anything. I don't need anything, but you.

I DON'T KNOW when I moved, but when the song ends, I'm standing in front of the stage staring up at my little swallow, drawn like a magnet to her presence. Story slips the guitar strap over her head.

"I don't need anything, but you." She sings the last song acapella. And then she drops off the front of the stage into my arms in a honeymoon carry.

The crowd cheers like mad.

Flynn scrambles to turn on his mic as I walk with Story to the back of the room. "That was Story Taylor. I'm Flynn, and we are the Storytellers. We'll be back after a little break, folks. Thanks for coming out."

I hum softly—the sound I make only for her. The way I call her name. She tucks her face into my neck and hums back.

"Thanks for coming for me," she murmurs.

Always, I want to say. I settle for humming some more.

"Does that mean always?" She reads my mind.

I nod and turn to kiss the top of her head. In the back corner, I tip her to her feet and crowd my body against hers,

196

shielding her from view from the rest of the bar. I point at her chest, then at mine.

Her smile flickers. There's still sadness around her. "I belong to you?"

I nod then reverse the order.

"You belong to me."

I nod again.

"Can I move in with you?"

A smile surprises my inexpressive face with its sudden appearance.

"Damn." She reaches up to place her palm against my cheek. "You are so handsome when you smile."

My smile widens.

"I'm sorry. I got scared."

I shake my head and point at myself, then give the sign for *sorry*.

"I know you're sorry. You never meant to hurt me. You were trying to take care of me."

I nod.

"I can't promise I won't freak out again."

I shake my head. I won't let you, I want to say. I point at my chest, then shake my head as I point out the door.

"You won't go?"

I nod.

"Never?"

I shake my head emphatically.

"You're mine?"

There's that smile again. My facial muscles will have to adjust to the new sensation.

"I love you."

I move in slowly, savoring every precious moment as I sip from her lips, gently at first, then moving into a possessive, claiming kiss.

Story relaxes more and more, the tension and cloud around her ebbing away.

I crook my finger, backing up a few steps to pull out a chair. Story immediately crawls into my lap, where she belongs.

CHAPTER 17

S *tory*
 "Catch me if you can!" I squeal the minute we climb out of the elevator at the Kremlin after my show. I take off running toward the door that leads to the roof.

I hear Oleg's soft chuckle right behind me, but he lets me pretend I'm getting away as I run up the stairs to the gorgeous rooftop pool. The air is freezing, and steam comes off the hot tub when I roll the cover up.

"Last one in is a rotten egg." I take off my clothes, giggling.

Oleg doesn't rush. He slowly strips, watching me with total absorption as I drop my coat, boots, tights, skirt, shirt, bra and panties onto the pebbled deck.

I jump in before I get cold and bob up and down, bouncing on my feet, making the water splash around my breasts as they dip in and out of the surface.

Oleg finishes undressing, looking like a stallion with a boner the size of my forearm. I splash him.

His eyes crinkle. He arches a brow and points a finger.

"Uh oh." I smile. "Is Big Daddy going to spank me?"

Pretty please.

I found out his other pet name for me—*shalun'ya*—means bad girl or minx, which I love. He descends into the water, standing on the first step, then sitting on the pool deck. His brows flick as he reaches for me.

Oh God.

He is going to spank me. I get fluttery and excited and a tiny bit nervous, only because last time it hurt almost as much as it felt good.

He parts his knees and pulls me across one of them, tipping me over so my hands rest on the pool deck behind him.

I let out a quavering *meep.*

He hums softly then smacks my wet ass.

"Ow! Oh my God, that hurts."

Another smack, served with a dark chuckle. I dance on my feet, thrilled. Horny. Smarting. He rubs my ass, then slides his fingers between my legs. I wriggle with the shock of sensation when his fingers brush my most sensitive bits. He delivers two more swift smacks then rubs some more.

Oh God, it's good.

So exciting. Delicious. The sharpness of the initial pain recedes as pleasure flushes through me. I don't know why I like this. It doesn't matter. It's Oleg, and I trust him completely.

He goes on for a few more rounds—a couple smacks, then his middle finger circling over my clit. My arousal ramps up swiftly. "More," I moan, even though my ass already stings.

Of course, he delivers, slapping me with seven rapid-fire spanks that make me squeal and kick my feet. And then we're suddenly both immersed in the water, warmth burning over the winter chill on my skin. Oleg pinches one nipple as he curls an arm behind my back and draws my body against his. I wrap my legs around his waist. He uses his hand to angle his cock to prod my entrance.

The water and weightlessness make it slippery and hard for him to get in, and a few moments later, I find myself on my knees on the step, my elbows on a cushion from a nearby chaise lounge, and Oleg pounding into me from behind. He grips my hair in his fist disrespectfully, and I love it. I love it because I know this man is the farthest thing from disrespectful outside of the bedroom. He's the safest scary I'll ever find, and I find his power and dominance delicious.

He rides me hard, protecting my hips from the side of the tub with his forearm around my waist. I lose my mind, crooning his name, panting, begging for release. His thumb finds my mouth. I suck it hard, hoping to bring him to climax, so I can have mine. It works. He growls and shoves in deep, bucking against my ass as he comes. I climax the moment he goes off, not needing the clit-rub he provides.

I scream because I can. Because it feels good to be as loud as I want up here on the roof.

When we both go still, Oleg's heart beating against my back, he lowers his lips to my ear and bites gently, then kisses.

I hear his soft hum—the sound he makes for me when we get close.

I make it back.

He pulls out and turns me around, pointing at my chest, then his.

"Yep, I say softly. I'm yours."

He arranges me in his lap in the water, still humming.

"Hey, guess what? We start our ASL class at the community college next month." I researched it yesterday and signed myself up. I would've signed Oleg up, too, but he needs to get registered first.

He raises his brows.

"We're both going to learn it, so we can talk easily. Otherwise, how are you going to talk to our kids?"

Oleg lets out a surprised puff of breath followed by a soft moan and blinks rapidly. If I didn't know better, I would swear my big strong man teared up. He points at me, then does the grabby-hand sign for *want,* then mimics rocking a baby.

"Yeah, I want kids, do you?"

Another soft moan and blinking. He nods.

"I'm thinking, like, three or four. A big noisy houseful of kids. Because crazy chaos is my jam."

Oleg laugh-sobs and leans his forehead against my cheek, rocking me gently in the water.

"Are you down."

He makes his humming sound and stands up, lifting me out of the water. He stoops to pick up his keycard, leaving our clothes on the deck as he carries me to the door.

"Where are we going? Are you going to fuck me again?" I'm not usually the dirty-talker, but after reading all the things Oleg wanted to say to me last week, I figure I'm voicing his thoughts.

His eyes go dark with wicked promise.

I giggle and tighten my hold on his neck, kicking my feet with delight.

EPILOGUE

*O*leg

"S-t-ory." I work carefully to make the sounds come off my lips right. I'm standing in the doorway of Story's music studio on the tenth floor where she teaches lessons and rehearses with the band.

Ravil got a speech therapist to work with me every week on learning to speak again. I make sounds with my lips to substitute for the sounds I can't speak with my tongue. I fucking hate the way it sounds, but seeing Story's face light up at hearing her name makes it worth it.

My girl whirls and smiles over her shoulder at me then takes a running leap, jumping into my arms. "Hi, Big Daddy," she says in a low, breathy voice.

Aw, fuck. Now I just want to press her back against the wall and give it to her hard, right here, right now.

But, no. I have other plans.

"How did speech therapy go?" she asks, dropping a dozen kisses over my face.

"Goov," I say. D's are still a work in progress. "Marry

me," I blurt. I'd just practiced an entire sentence for an hour, but I buckled under pressure.

Story's head jerks back to look at my face. "Did you just propose?"

"Yes. Will you?" The words don't quite sound right, but she understands me.

She laugh-cries. "Yes. Yes, I will."

I shift my hands to produce the ring I tucked in my pocket and show it to her. It's a small, delicate ring with three slender diamond-encrusted bands braided together and three half-carat diamonds on top. Story's not the type to want a big rock or anything too flashy. I wanted something artsy and sweet, like her.

"I love it." She lets me slip it on her ring finger. "I love it so much."

"Come on." I carry her out of the music studio and into the elevator. When we get out, I go in the main entrance to the penthouse where everyone is waiting.

The assholes all heard me practicing for the last hour, so everyone knew it was coming.

"Well?" Sasha demands. Maxim holds a bottle of champagne in his hands, the cork ready to pop.

"Yes," I say. I don't put my *lastochka* down. Carrying her around is one of the biggest pleasures of my life.

The room explodes into cheers and whoops. Even baby Benjamin cheers and claps his chubby hands. The cork pops and hits the ceiling. Champagne spills on the floor.

"*Pozdravleniya!*" Sasha shouts her congratulations in Russian. Pavel, Dima and Nikolia repeat it, followed by Lucy, who has learned basic Russian faster than any of us learned English. Pavel's girlfriend, Kayla is visiting from L.A. and she bounces up and down, as perky as she is sweet.

Maxim pours two glasses of champagne and passes them to us. We wait until everyone has a glass.

"To Story, who revealed our brother Oleg to us." Ravil lifts his glass.

"To Story." I raise mine.

"I love you," Story says to me then twists in my arms. "I love all of you." She lifts her glass, then sips it. "You're the best new adopted family I could have, and I love living here with you, but I understand if you have to kick us out after our second or third kid."

There's laughter and more banter, but I don't hear any of it because the world narrows to Story for me, like it always does.

My obsession. My beautiful swallow.

And soon, my wife.

THE END

THANK you for reading *The Enforcer*! If you enjoyed it, I would so appreciate your review. They make a huge difference for indie authors. Sign up for my newsletter to get word of the next Chicago Bratva books!

WANT FREE RENEE ROSE BOOKS?

Dressmaker's and *Her Billionaire Boss*. In addition to the free stories, you will also get special pricing, exclusive previews and news of new releases.

OTHER TITLES BY RENEE ROSE

Chicago Bratva

"Prelude" in Black Light: Roulette War

The Director

The Fixer

"Owned" in Black Light: Roulette Rematch

The Enforcer

Vegas Underground Mafia Romance

King of Diamonds

Mafia Daddy

Jack of Spades

Ace of Hearts

Joker's Wild

His Queen of Clubs

Dead Man's Hand

Wild Card

More Mafia Romance

Her Russian Master

The Don's Daughter

Mob Mistress

The Bossman

Contemporary

Daddy Rules Series

Fire Daddy

Hollywood Daddy

Stepbrother Daddy

Master Me Series

Her Royal Master

Her Russian Master

Her Marine Master

Yes, Doctor

Double Doms Series

Theirs to Punish

Theirs to Protect

Holiday Feel-Good

Scoring with Santa

Saved

Other Contemporary

Black Light: Valentine Roulette

Black Light: Roulette Redux

Black Light: Celebrity Roulette

Black Light: Roulette War

Black Light: Roulette Rematch

Punishing Portia (written as Darling Adams)

The Professor's Girl

Safe in his Arms

Paranormal

Wolf Ranch Series

Rough

Wild

Feral

Savage

Fierce

Ruthless

Wolf Ridge High Series

Alpha Bully

Alpha Knight

Bad Boy Alphas Series

Alpha's Temptation

Alpha's Danger

Alpha's Prize

Alpha's Challenge

Alpha's Obsession

Alpha's Desire

Alpha's War

Alpha's Mission

Alpha's Bane

Alpha's Secret

Alpha's Prey

Alpha's Sun

Shifter Ops

Alpha's Moon

Alpha's Vow

Alpha's Revenge

Midnight Doms

Alpha's Blood

His Captive Mortal

Alpha Doms Series

The Alpha's Hunger

The Alpha's Promise

The Alpha's Punishment

Other Paranormal

The Winter Storm: An Ever After Chronicle

Sci-Fi

Zandian Masters Series

His Human Slave

His Human Prisoner

Training His Human

His Human Rebel

His Human Vessel

His Mate and Master

Zandian Pet

Their Zandian Mate

His Human Possession

Zandian Brides

Night of the Zandians

Bought by the Zandians

Mastered by the Zandians

Zandian Lights

Kept by the Zandian

Claimed by the Zandian

Stolen by the Zandian

Other Sci-Fi

The Hand of Vengeance

Her Alien Masters

Regency

The Darlington Incident

Humbled

The Reddington Scandal

The Westerfield Affair

Pleasing the Colonel

Western

His Little Lapis

The Devil of Whiskey Row

The Outlaw's Bride

Medieval

Mercenary

Medieval Discipline

Lords and Ladies

The Knight's Prisoner

Betrothed

Held for Ransom

The Knight's Seduction

The Conquered Brides (5 book box set)

Renaissance

Renaissance Discipline

ABOUT RENEE ROSE

USA TODAY BESTSELLING AUTHOR RENEE ROSE loves a dominant, dirty-talking alpha hero! She's sold over a million copies of steamy romance with varying levels of kink. Her books have been featured in USA Today's *Happily Ever After* and *Popsugar*. Named Eroticon USA's Next Top Erotic Author in 2013, she has also won *Spunky and Sassy's* Favorite Sci-Fi and Anthology author, *The Romance Reviews* Best Historical Romance, and *has* hit the *USA Today* list seven times with her Wolf Ranch series and various anthologies.

Please follow her on:
  Bookbub | Goodreads

Renee loves to connect with readers!
www.reneeroseromance.com
reneeroseauthor@gmail.com

Printed in the USA
CPSIA information can be obtained
at www.ICGtesting.com
LVHW051543171123
764112LV00071B/2696